MW01121182

THE SECOND COMING OF AGE
Liberty and Justice

Curtiss DeVedrine

Writers Club Press
San Jose New York Lincoln Shanghai

The Second Coming of Age
Liberty and Justice

Published by Writers Club Press
an imprint of iUniverse.com, Inc.

For information address:
iUniverse.com, Inc.
620 North 48th Street
Suite 201
Lincoln, NE 68504-3467
www.iuniverse.com

ISBN: 0-595-09150-4

Printed in the United States of America

Contents

Foreword

Anyone can write a book of fiction, though I truly believe that great storytellers are a special breed, which I'm not. This book was not a conscious effort to gain fame or wealth, but in fact could well defame me or, worse, those who love me. For this I apologize in advance for any injury or embarrassment that this book may cause any human, living or dead. And for those who do take offense to my story. I hope they find it in their hearts to forgive any ignorance or short-sightedness that may have misguided me. Surely you are wondering after such an apology why I would even bother to go on with a story, or even more pertinent why you should occupy your precious time on its mere words.

About 1703 at Chateau Dosey Vedrine, a vineyard in Southern France, Jean Baptist my sixth great-grandfather of direct lineage was born into a noble family. Being a second-son he would not inherit the larger portion of the estate, as custom of the time allowed him only the choice to become a Catholic priest or to join the military. Why Jean chose the military is a mystery as his younger brother became a priest, but Jean did choose the military and so you are reading this.

Jean's service to France, which at that time was building empires, brought him to the New World to what is now Illinois and to the French and Indian Wars. About the age of fifty-five, as he was retiring from service as an officer, he married Elizabeth De Monchervaux, a young daughter of a fellow officer. Elizabeth's mother was a Native American woman, the daughter of a tribal chief an ally to France. My grandfather Jean, and his half French bride Elizabeth had many children whom they dearly loved and proudly passed on their heritage. Even as a tiny boy five generations later, I can still recall the moment my mother whispered into my ear our family secret.

There you have it, not all, but enough to let you know that this fictional story is about a real family's secret kept for six generations. It was the inspiration for this book, I pray that you can find pleasure in reading it, if only a fraction as much as I take in sharing it with you.

JUST ANOTHER DAY IN NEW ORLEANS

October

"Talk to me, Johnny," a voice said. But Johnny couldn't hear it. The last time Johnny had looked at his watch it'd been 3:33 a.m. At least two hours before he would leave. Wondering if he could stay awake, it seemed doubtful at this moment. Youthful energy levels had begun fading lately. Even staying alive had become another burden.

Don't worry, he often thought, about things that couldn't be changed. The old adage had served him well in earlier years. Now it had become a meaningless cliche', an excuse to maintain the status quo. Status quo seemed to be all there was left in life and even that was denigrating with the passing of the years. A gnawing feeling eating on the lining of the stomach was slowly replacing the joy of life. In the beginning it had been dismissed as queasiness or as indigestion, but with each passing day it made itself more known and unwelcome.

It was the feeling a person perceives when they first fall in love, the heart calling out even before the head knows. It was the language of emotion, something the intellect can only guess at, poke at and fumble with in the dark. A sacred language of the heart translated by the painful acknowledgment of fears or failures and soothed by being brutally honest about one's purpose in life. An early warning of a sacrifice to come, payments due to maintain sanity. It did not care what the price would be, it demanded fulfillment at any cost. It had no regard for tradition, custom, or rules of law, it only knew what it needed.

Denying a call from the heart is a futile human effort. It is to deny the existence of a greater power. To hold on to life's status quo was only a mirage. Appearing safer for the moment on the outside, while it slowly destroyed from the inside. If practiced long enough, it could totally consume its practitioner, searing the conscience, wounding the soul. In the grand scheme, the only thing that stayed the same, was that nothing ever stayed the same.

Johnny had plans, there had always been plans. Since childhood his life had been planned, charted, and tracked by his parents. Earn a university degree, get married, raise a family, and work for the brass ring of retirement. Johnny had never questioned the sensibility of the plans, most everyone worked off the same basic sets of plans. He had earned a degree and had something like a career, but he had never gotten around to the wife and children.

His feet slipped out from under him on the wet iron stairs. Day dreaming while walking, he had not held onto the handrail as safety guideline 22-55 had instructed. His body had tumbled down the stairs until finally coming to rest upside down. Limp and unmoving, he could have been mistaken as a dead man. Rapidly and instinctively, his mind took an inventory of his body parts as large secretions of adrenaline raced through his veins. The feeling of panic forced his mouth to run dry as he held his breath waiting for the pain to begin.

"All present and accounted for," he said aloud to no one. His thumb ached as he tried to regain his footing. Probably not broken, it did not hurt badly enough, talking to himself as though his voice were a consoling doctor. Large drops of driving rain pelted his face and eyelids, stinging on impact and tickling as they ran down his neck. He felt as though he would drown in the sea of driving rain if he didn't find shelter soon.

Millions of simultaneous impacts of earth's most valuable resource slammed hard against the metal surfaces. Gravity commanding them to race for the lowest point on earth since the very instant of their birth. Weakly Johnny unraveled his legs and crawled to his knees checking the surveillance cameras that pointed away from him momentarily. His lungs convulsed instinctively expelling the unwelcome moisture that had seeped in as he lay on his back.

Johnny knew people who lived apparently fulfilled lives, holding a job and raising children. Most people did. He had never had any children and knew he'd missed out. He also knew that many helpless people in the world were suffering from disease and starvation, while at the same time the world's middle class and wealthy bought luxuries like air conditioning instead of sharing resources that could have saved the lives of innocent children.

Prosperous self-proclaimed, born-again hypocrites, or Hypochristians as Johnny thought of them, worshiped their consumer idols in overbuilt churches. They were the people who disappointed Johnny the most. They pursued self-serving egocentric value systems to justify egomaniac quest for spiritual and material superiority. They politely ignored less fortunate people as less deserving. Johnny knew that he was as guilty as anyone, believers and unbelievers alike. He was the hypocrite he knew best. Tragedies and catastrophes were all over the newspapers, television, and radio. The human race for material comfort was destroying the world and had finally brought it to the brink.

Irresponsible stewarding and misuse of natural resources had compromised everyone, the poor and helpless suffering first. Polluting the atmosphere, depleting the ozone layer, inorganic farming, destruction of forest and freshwater habitats, depletion of the ocean's fisheries, negligent dumping of waste, those and countless other forms of carelessness had finally overpowered the earth's ability to regenerate itself and to provide. Now putting food and comfort into the homes of the highest bidders had become a mechanized death march.

Shortsighted profit driven economies thrived on degrading the environment. Responsibility to store, dispose of, or recycle waste and by-products were handed off to companies with little too lose if they damaged the environment. Often polluting the environment was legal, with young engineers graduating from major universities singing, "The solution to pollution is dilution." After all, who lobbied lawmakers? Who paid for high dollar election campaigns? Who paid attention? Did anyone care? Was anyone going to stop it before it was too late? Probably not, not until all fisheries were declared dangerous to human health and starving had become a worldwide holocaust, Johnny had begun to believe.

The surveillance camera was turning in its slow circle. Johnny slipped behind a concrete column to avoid being spotted and instinctively looked around for any other cameras in the area. Years of working around restricted environments monitored by security cameras and sensors had instilled a constant quest for privacy.

Johnny had come to believe that greed, ignorance, and the lack of character in the so-called ruling moral majority were the largest contributors to the ecological collapse. Industrialized nations were too comfortable to worry, still managing to ignore the growing signs of revolution from planet Earth. Johnny wanted to leave the world a better place than he'd found it. Perhaps the feeling began as a Boy Scout or during his Christian upbringing. Maybe watching the Lone Ranger as a kid, but wherever the inspiration had come from, Johnny felt certain he was failing as a human being.

"Goofy," he told himself out loud. "Why do I load myself up with these feelings of guilt? I'm decent, I'm as good as the next person." He did not believe he could wipe out greed or ignorance, single handedly, but he wanted to apply himself to something worthwhile. He usually consoled himself by thinking things would have been different if he had been born in different circumstances, made different choices.

"Johnny, come in, Johnny," the radio voice said again. Johnny thought he'd heard something and looked around.

He wanted to take better care of himself. Most of his adult life he had eaten out of tin cans or in fast food joints, but lately, he had begun taking vitamins and eating organic food at home. He didn't really believe eating healthier fare would make him live any longer, but it did make him feel better about himself. He had passed up opportunities to marry intelligent women, never able to make a commitment. All of his women friends had eventually married, finally giving up on him. Nowadays his life was a continuous cycle of work and sleep. A few diversions a couple of times a year broke the monotony. He knew he was a workaholic biding his time until retirement.

Occasionally he found himself standing in the hallways at work, staring at pictures of retired men from years gone by. Their faces were old and tired, and none of them appeared interested or even very capable of doing much of anything. Sadly, he knew that most of the retired people in his line of work died within ten years, their life spans shortened by decades of sleep deprivation.

"Johnny, talk to me, Johnny," the blaring two-way radio broadcast blasted again. He maneuvered the stairs holding on to the slippery metal handrails. Six-inch deep rainwater puddles surrounded an old corroded building. Blowing wind and rain whipped through the doorway and between the cracks in the walls, drenching the paperwork and equipment. Johnny lifted the crude canvas flap hanging over the doorway and set his chemical-soiled and slimy leather gloves on the counter. Water dripped off the end of his nose and off the lobes of his ears as he dug through his rain suit to find the two-way radio microphone.

"Johnny, talk to me, Johnny," The radio repeated. He tried to get his throbbing thumb to squeeze the radio microphone talk button.

"Hey, go ahead," Johnny yelled above the thunderclap that shook the sides of the shed, the fluorescent light flickered off and on. Rain dripping in from the leaking roof ran down his neck and seeped down the collar of his raincoat. His clothes were soaked as though he had on no rain suit and he shivered against the dampness, trying to warm up.

"Johnny, we have been calling you for half an hour, are you all right?" the radio voice said.

"Yeah, fine. I couldn't hear your transmissions above all the noise out here," he said.

"We need you to go up and check the system. Our poison gas detectors are in alarm." The radio voice ordered him. Johnny blew the water out of his mustache in an effort to respond more clearly.

"All right, I'm headed that way," Johnny said. The wind and rain slapped at the sides of the shed as he deliberately left the microphone dangling out of the collar of his raincoat. He walked back out of the artificial lighting, back into the storm where the rain had been falling nonstop for days. He recited a prayer as he walked between the humming, vibrating, high-pressure piping screaming with boiling nerve gas. Johnny had often wondered what was done with all of it. Who was going to be killed with it, and for what reasons?

Johnny approached the leak from the down wind side and could smell the chemical's bite before he could see it. The poisonous fog engulfed him in a gust of wind, choked him, and forced him to run for fresh air holding his breath. He stopped at a ten-foot-tall electrified wire perimeter fence, designed to keep unauthorized persons outside and nerve gas plant employees on the job. The fence was topped with four rows of razor-sharp barbed wire and electronic sensors that alarmed the security guards of anyone's location should they touch the fence. Johnny avoided the fence and picked up the microphone.

"Hey, Tee Boy," he called. Tee Boy was a person who sat at main frame computer system located in an explosion proof, gas proof, air-tight safe haven building with three-foot thick concrete and steel walls. Nine computer monitor screens and six key boards kept the plant producing noxious nerve gas, twenty four hours a day, 365 days a year.

"We've got a bad leak," Johnny said. "Looks like a lightning strike has ruptured the piping, I can't get close to it. We're going to have to shut the whole plant down and quickly! Call the State Police and

OSHA, the vapor cloud is heading across the interstate. We're going to be lucky if we don't kill a host of innocent people." Johnny's adrenaline was pumping.

"Johnny, are you sure? We don't want to cause a panic?" Tee Boy said. Johnny ran further up wind to get away from the gas.

"Tee Boy, listen to me," Johnny said. "I'm telling you for the second time. We've got a bad leak and if you don't start evacuating people right away, it's going to turn into a disaster. It may already be too late."

He climbed out of the shower, dressed back into his street clothes, and climbed into his car. It was late in the morning and the sun was already up over the city. Poisonous gas fumes still reeked in his freshly washed hair. He checked his face and neck in the car's rearview mirror for chemical burns and found only a small red spot, on his chin.

His lungs concerned him though. Taking deep breaths caused pain and forced him to cough. It wasn't the first time he'd breathed the nerve gas. Johnny would wait until shift change that night to report the inhalation. That is if it didn't get worse and if he didn't have to go to the hospital. Tee Boy would be angry with him either way.

"One of these days, I'll never have to go back in there," Johnny assured himself, under his breath. He stood by his opened car door as guards at the plant exit searched under the seats, in the glove compartment and through the trunk. He was surprised, they didn't have him undress.

"All right, you can leave now," the sadistic looking guard said.

Johnny climbed into his car, let out on the clutch. Driving through the security gates, he turned left down the pot-holed road and out onto the busy highway. The same road he'd driven home a thousand times before. Sipping on a steaming hot cup of coffee, he maneuvered through the early morning traffic. Carefully he avoided the holes in the road and spilled coffee on himself. People rushed to work speeding past his car. The morning sky was cloudless, clear, blue, and brilliant. The rising sun stabbed his sleep-dilated eyes as he dug in the glove box for his sunglasses. Tilting the car's visor down lower barely blocked the merciless sun. He tossed the empty paper coffee cup on the floor and surveyed the pile of trash that had accumulated there. The car was in bad need of a car wash. Leaning forward in his seat he rubbed his eyes and turned the radio to his favorite morning program. Public Radio International was giving the morning market report. The news that the Dow Jones Industrial stocks were rising brought a little color back into his pale sunlight-deprived cheeks. The faster the stock market went up, the sooner Johnny could retire. He hoped to be able to take early retirement at age sixty. For fifteen years he had driven in and out of those plant gates dreading it more with each passing day. Once upon a time, he had been a sales representative spending most of his days on the road, taking clients out to eat, play golf, or make sales presentations. An economic downturn and disillusionment with his product line had forced him to find another job. Working in the nerve gas plant was the only job he found that paid him nearly as well as sales and believing in your product's value to the world wasn't a job requirement. As the years flew by his hopes of finding any job that improved the human condition grew slimmer, further dashing his hopes of a happier future.

His mind flashed back to the days fresh out of college. He had pitched minor league baseball, believing he would break into the major leagues where he would make a fortune, marry his college sweetheart, and live happily ever after. Those dreams faded quickly the day he'd torn his shoulder in an automobile accident. He had never been able to forgive himself or the drunkened driver who had caused the wreck. His fiancee did not hang around long after he had been released from the hospital, claiming she was moving to New York to pursue a career. She had met a Wall Street stockbroker and married within six months. Johnny had never really gotten over her.

This morning's ride home, sixty miles one way, was the worst one in recent memory. Pulling off the Interstate he drove into a Waffle House restaurant parking lot and stumbled through the door. At the counter by the cash register, on his usual stool he flopped down. Neon lights glared. A smiling waitress brought him a cup of black coffee without his asking for it. He tried to smile back at her. Sipping his too hot coffee, the aroma and steam drifting up his nostrils he wondered why he didn't get a real house closer to his job. He doubted he'd ever take the sailboat he called home to the Caribbean after he retired anyway.

"Johnny, you look like you had a hard night at work," the waitress said. He smiled back at her over the menu, too drunk from the lack of sleep to form a sentence. She was used to it. "You're coming through here a couple of hours later than usual." He stared at the menu still trying to smile again. Nothing looked good this morning but he knew from experience if he ate now he'd get a second wind. She stood now across the counter from him, pen and pad in hand. Her hair was pulled up under her uniform cap. Tired now herself from covering the night shift she had waited longer than usual to leave hoping Johnny would come in.

"Clovis, give me one of those little boxes of cereal please," he said. She prepared his cereal for him polishing his spoon on her white apron before setting it on a folded paper napkin. Johnny poured the cereal into the bowl and used the glass of milk to fill it. He centered everything on the polished counter top in front of him and began eating.

"Picky, picky, picky," Clovis mumbled under her breath as she walked away.

Clovis was thirty-five years of age and had two young children at home. Her husband had left her and the children three years back and had sent some child support when he was working, which wasn't very often or very much. She hated leaving her children at the babysitter's all night while she worked. Most of the time she got home in the morning just in time to get them off to school. It was a miserable life for her, but at least they were all healthy, and her kids appeared to be happy.

Clovis knew that Johnny was single and had a regular job. That he was also polite, kind, and nice looking was the icing on the cake. Fact was Clovis would have done almost anything to get him interested in her, but he had never taken any of her hints seriously. Occasionally he had returned her flirting, but he had never followed through with the offer of a date. At least he left twenty percent tips, Clovis thought. Few customers did that.

"Yeah, this bad weather made everything wrong last night," he said. "We had to shut down the operation before I could go home."

Clovis tried to give him as much attention as she could while she waited on her other customers. She believed that Johnny, being a bachelor all his life, had been a terrible waste of a life, and she still felt that she could make him into a wonderful husband and father. Johnny gulped down his black coffee as soon as it cooled down a little, and Clovis refilled it without asking.

She chit chatted between serving other customers about how much trouble she was having with her older boy at school, Johnny finished his cereal, dropped some money on the counter and rose to go. He told her thanks without looking to see if she'd heard him. Slipping on his dark sunglasses he walked back out into the parking lot and unlocked his car. It was covered with residue from the poison gas plant.

By the time he got to his boat at the Marina Del Ray in the Tchefuncta River at Madisonville, Louisiana, it was midmorning. His alarm clock would go off at 2:30 that afternoon, then he would have to start the process all over again. Work shifts were normally based on a total of fifteen days a month, but he had been forced to work a month of night shifts. This would be his third week in a row without a day off.

Shaving in his boat's tiny teak wood bathroom, he cut the corners of his mustache and his side burns evenly. He didn't know how he was going to do it, but he wanted somehow to find another way to earn a living.

Johnny considered himself nearing middle age and had almost given up making a difference in the world. Getting home safely after working all night seemed hard enough. If he could finish this forced overtime, he had two weeks of vacation to look forward to and planned to meet his buddy Lee in Gulf Shores, Alabama.

FLORIDA, WASHINGTON, D.C. AND LOUISIANA

Virginia Forest put the last monkey in the cage at the primate center, latched the cage door, and checked her watch. All of her staff had gone home on time and, as usual, she was trying to get a head start on the next day. Supervising six employees was not an easy job, but she really enjoyed working with the animals. After working for a vet just out of college, she landed this job at the primate center in Pensacola, Florida. The pay was decent and there were health benefits, so the years slowly passed. Supporting her six-year-old son and her disabled husband left little room for aspirations.

Virginia's husband Michael was an American Indian, who once had a promising career as a military physician. Leaving the reservation, he'd joined the U.S. military when they agreed to send him through college. In the beginning, he kept his ambition to be a doctor secret from everyone, especially his family, until he'd proven to himself that he could achieve his goal. Once he graduated and repaid the military by serving year for year as a military doctor, he planned to go back to his reservation and open a free clinic.

A few years after finishing medical school he had been diagnosed with brain cancer. He never told Virginia of his suspicions, but he personally believed he had been a casualty of a military experiment, in the hospital where he had served his residency. During that first year, Michael had been naive enough to volunteer in several "supposably" safe experiments. Later he realized he had been a human guinea pig. Within three months of being diagnosed, Michael had been reduced to a near vegetable state, leaving behind a tiny son and a devoted grieving wife.

Taking care of primates wasn't the only thing that was occupying Virginia's mind that evening. She had to get to the babysitter's to pick up her son soon or she'd be late again. The sitter had warned her just the week before that she would begin charging a late fee the next time Virginia picked Naichie up late. The telephone rang in Virginia's office, just as she was locking the front door and she quickly unlocked the door and grabbed the telephone. Expecting to hear the babysitter's voice reminding her to be on time, she heard a different voice.

"Virginia Forest speaking, can I help you?" she said.

"Virginia, this is Reba McGinty," the voice said.

"Reba, I haven't heard from you since two Christmases ago. How's your mom?" Virginia asked. Checking her watch again, she was going to have to call Reba back.

"Mom's great. How are you doing?" Reba replied.

"I'm doing great, Reba, but can I call you when I get home?" Virginia said. "I've got to get to the sitter's house, quickly."

"Yes that's fine, I just wanted you to know that I'm coming to visit you in a couple of weeks," Reba said.

"Wonderful," Virginia said. "Call me tonight." Virginia sped her white Ford Expedition out of the primate center parking lot and headed to the babysitter's. She was ten minutes late, as usual, but this time the sitter didn't appear to notice. Naichie was always delighted to see his mother, gave her a strong hug and ran outside without waiting for her. Virginia met Naichie at the truck and helped him get in. On the way home they made their usual fast food stop.

Just before dark, Virginia and Naichie pulled up to their small farmhouse at the end of the road, where their Tennessee Walker horses gathered at the fence to greet them and to await the evening's ration of sweet feed. Mother and son got out of the truck and walked toward the barn holding hands, enjoying the orange and pink sunset sky which gave the indian summer pasture and the pecan trees a warm iridescent glow. Naichie took the feed bucket off the large rusty nail in the feed room and filled it to the brim, careful not to drop any on the dirt floor as he measured the sticky feed. A mouse jumped out of the feed barrel just before Naichie replaced the metal lid and scampered behind the saddles. Naichie looked behind the saddles, probing for the small mammal.

Wrestling the heaping bucket out of the feed room, Naichie spilled a little on the ground as he walked toward the horses. Ducks ran in and out gobbling the grain, quacking, squabbling amongst themselves, and blocking the access to the stalls. Naichie pushed his small legs through, while his mother concealed her delight as his face radiated determination. His efforts were deliberate, concealing his fear of the aggressive honking birds, awkwardly waddling in at half his height.

In each horse's stall, Naichie poured the sweet feed, and the horses greedily consumed the long awaited, twice a day ration while Virginia and Naichie petted and curry-combed the smooth summer coats, the horses shone from the care selflessly given by their loving human keepers. This was an evening routine where all involved delighted in love and quality time. Mother and son shared the day's joys and failures with each other, recharging their own emotional batteries.

"Mama," Naichie said. "I think my horse is smaller than she used to be. Could she be shrinking, you know, like old people do?" Naichie was tip toeing, reaching as high as he could on the horse, combing near the withers. Virginia smiled down into Naichie's beautiful dark brown eyes and earnest face. She patted his head, a hesitant witness to the boy's rapid growth.

"Naichie, Sugar isn't getting any smaller. You're getting taller," Virginia said. The fact brought tears to her eyes. He looked up at his mother, then down at his own legs. Virginia stood waiting for the expression of his reaction to this obvious revelation.

"Mom, will I get as big as Daddy?" Naichie asked. Virginia, barely able to hold back her tears, looked into Naichie's little boy eyes.

"Yes, my beautiful son, you will be a strong man like your father was," Virginia said. She wiped the dampness off her face with the long sleeve of her green lab coat. Naichie didn't seem to notice.

"Senator, the Bureau of Land Management is on line one," the secretary said. The intercoms little speaker fell silent waiting for his reply. Senator Richard Redhead from the state of California shook Dan Yamaha's hand and walked him toward the impressive paneled lobby. Anyone looking on would have believed them to be old and good friends. They walked through the heavy dark wooden double doors that kept the uninitiated out of the Senator's office. Once again they faced each other, their outreached hands connected and their eyes locked in an unexpressed knowing of their mutual need for one another. A parasite upon a parasite.

"Dan, I don't want you to worry about your supply of redwood timber or any other lumber for that matter. I am very aware of your company's needs, how you depend on our timber and of the money your company contributes back every year to our political party. We won't let you down," Senator Redhead said. "The Bureau of Land Management is cutting a new road through the middle of those northern virgin redwoods. Your people should be able to send logging crews into any part of those National Park lands by the middle of next year."

The two men shook hands again. Dan Yamaha smiled and walked through the lobby door. Senator Redhead smiled his professional smile masking any personal thoughts and stepped inside his office closing the door behind him. Opening the twenty or so folded hundred dollar bills Dan had slipped into his palm as they shook hands. Dick smiled again, even more broadly this time, then walked back to his office telephone and picked up on line one. The telephone tap detector flashed green, meaning the line was clean.

"Hello, this is Senator Redhead," he said.

"Hello Senator, this is Mike Mills," he said. "We received your instructions on the redwood reserve road. Senator, I'm sorry but the Bureau of Land Management can't justify building those roads."

"Why the hell not, Mills?" the Senator replied. He growled in his most intimidating voice.

"Sir, we just do not have the money, and we wouldn't do it if we had the money," Mills said.

"Why wouldn't you do it if you had the money Mills?" the Senator said. He spoke more quietly now as his face got redder than the remaining frizzy hair on his slick, sweating head. His too large ears, freckled and age spotted, stuck awkwardly out on the sides.

"Senator, with all due respect, the money we would receive for cutting down that ancient virgin forest wouldn't even cover the cost of the roads we'd have to build to get in there," Mills said. "And we don't have a dime to spare in our budget."

"Mr. Mills, as you know, I am Chairman of the Finance Committee that oversees your budget. I guarantee that you will get those moneys and your people will build those roads. To hell with your cost justification, do you understand?" the Senator yelled into the receiver then cleared his throat. The telephone was silent for a moment as Mills reconsidered his options.

"Yes sir, I understand completely. We'll have to send in surveyors before we can get started," Mills said. He hated politics and politicians.

You couldn't live with them and you couldn't kill them, he thought almost out loud.

"Listen to me Mills, I advise you to get started on that road right away," Senator Redhead said. "I want those roads finished by early summer. I won't take any excuses very kindly."

Thirty years ago, as a freshman politician, Senator Richard Redhead thought he would be able to make a difference in the United States. He believed however small a contribution it might finally be, the United States would be a better place because he had been a good Senator. Possibly, he secretly hoped, he might even earn himself a place in the history books, as one of the greater men ever to have graced the Nation's Capital. However, somewhere in the business of doing business, his belief of being a servant to the American people had gotten lost in the shuffle of his need to be reelected. Raising campaign contributions and scratching "Capitol Hill Backs" now occupied most of his working time.

"Yes sir, I'll get started on it right away," Mills said. He hung up the telephone. "Remind me to kick my dog when I get home," he told his assistant. The assistant gave Mills a blank wondering stare, Mills told him, never mind.

"Too much damned red tape in Washington," Senator Redhead said to himself after he hung up a telephone. "You can hardly get things done anymore. Damned New Aged Communist Green People environmentalists are hiding in all the cracks." Photographs of famous world figures shaking the Senators hand smiled down on Dick as he stared out the window into the pouring rain.

"Senator, the vote that allows foreign entities to continue mining minerals off Federal Lands is coming up in twenty minutes," the receptionist was speaking again over the intercom. The Senator checked his watch while the wind blew acid rain horizontally outside his window.

"Sarah, get me that file and get me Senator Fred McKenny on the phone," Senator Redhead said. The receptionist got Senator McKenny on the telephone and transferred the call to Senator Redhead's office. Senator Redhead picked up the telephone and spoke.

"Fred, this is Dick, do we have any major opposition to this mineral extraction bill?" Senator Redhead said. He was suddenly tired and hoped to take a nap soon.

"No sir Senator, there is a tiny opposition backed only by the Green Earth Movement. But I've got confirmations from at least seventy-five senators, it's going to go through with no problems," Senator McKenny said. "After all, nothing on this bill is changing, we're just renewing old policy. You know, business as usual."

Lee Johnson stepped up to the 18th hole tee box at Mallard Cove Golf Course. He took his favorite driver out of the well-organized designer bag of this year's most popular clubs, then tapped his spiked golf shoes to get off any loose dirt. Planting his feet in the well-groomed soft green turf he turned and smiled over his shoulder at Paul Saul, just before he took his back swing.

"Hey, pretty Paul, I've got a wager for you," Lee said. "If I lay this ball on the green in two strokes, you'll fix my speeding ticket?" Paul Saul, the District Attorney, looked at Lee and nodded his head in agreement. He flipped his cellular phone closed, then slid it into his shirt pocket and extended his hand, palm up, toward Lee. With an election-winning smile, he looked into Lee's eyes.

"And if you don't lay it on the green in two strokes, what do I get?" Paul asked.

"I'll take you and your wife to the casino for dinner," Lee said. Paul smiled, Lee swung and laid the ball within ten yards of the 18th green on the first stroke. He turned and smiled broadly at Paul, but didn't say a word.

"How about you take me out to eat anyway?" Paul said smiling. Lee reached into his shirt pocket and handed the speeding ticket into Paul's open hand.

"It's a deal," Lee said. Carefully Paul stepped up to the tee, placed his ball, and swung. His ball landed about twenty yards behind Lee's ball. Lee looked at Paul and chuckled. Paul shook his head in disappointment, he'd only won once against Lee, and he had been sure Lee had thrown the game on purpose.

"Paul, your game is a little off today, huh?" Lee chuckled, then climbed back into the golf cart. Paul climbed in beside him and checked his watch.

"Just about time to call it a day," Paul said. "I wonder what my wife's serving for dinner?"

Lee drove back out toward home alone thinking about the golf game with Paul. He should have mentioned the real estate deal to Paul today, but the speeding ticket needed to be fixed before his court date on the first of the month.

"Oh well, next week during our regular Wednesday game," Lee said out loud to no one, he would ask Paul then. Lee pulled up to Eric Muller's construction shop and walked through to the office. Eric stood and turned to shake Lee's hand as he came through the door.

"Hey Eric, how's the subdivision coming along?" Lee asked. Eric hung up the telephone back on its base. The desk was made of handmade cypress, with perfect lines, and joinery. Eric was a man of perfection and it showed in everything he touched.

"Good things keep falling from the sky," Eric said. "I just hung the phone up with the CEO of Century Colonial. They're building retirement communities across the nation. They want to buy a piece of our lake subdivision, near the back, to build one of their assisted living communities." Lee tried to read Eric's face. Eric smiled back at him.

"What are they offering?" Lee asked.

"Fifty thousand per acre," Eric said. "They want ten acres." Eric smiled again at Lee.

"That's half a million," Lee said. "We didn't give but one million for the entire 100 acres," Lee said. The two men smiled at each other. "Maybe we could talk them into buying 25 acres? Then we could develop this whole subdivision with their money."

"I tried, but he said that they're only interested in 10 acres," Eric said. "I told him I was fairly sure the partners would go for it, that I would let him know by Monday."

"Yeah right, don't let that one slip away," Lee said.

"I figure we'll be able to squeeze them for a hundred grand more," Eric said, grinning.

Lee hopped into his car and rode toward his house down the twisting and turning River Road. His car squealed around the corners as he pushed it up to its limits of speed and handling. There would be no dinner waiting for him, no smiling wife to greet him at the door, no energetic children to brighten his evening, only Cadillac, his big fat black cat, would greet him at the door tonight. Early the next day he would rise when Cadillac woke him for breakfast then drive the six hours from Lake Charles to Gulf Shores.

AN ANNUAL EVENT IN GULF
SHORES, ALABAMA @ THE
FLORABAMA

How Lucky Can You Get?

Gulf Shores, Alabama, was known lovingly as the Red Neck Rivera, a primary summer vacation spot for families living in the Southeast United States. Since the 80's the tourist population had grown so quickly condominiums and hotels now hid the beachfront.

Johnny drove out to Gulf Shores from Madisonville, taking the usual half a day to get there. Stopping at antique shops along the way he finally pulled his car into the freshly mowed, pine tree shaded front yard of Lee's trailer. Lee sat on the porch, in a white plastic lawn chair sweating, smoking his usual ultra light cigarette. Streams of perspiration had formed tracks through the dust on his face, beginning at his graying hair, and muddying up on the collar of his white knit designer golf shirt. His bright white teeth shown at Johnny across the yard.

Lee didn't allow anyone to smoke inside of his trailer. He didn't like the smell of stale smoke, but he was addicted to the nicotine, so even he smoked outside. Johnny climbed out of the car, grabbed his backpack, and walked up the weathered wooden steps to the porch. He ducked a little to keep from hitting his head on the low porch roof.

"You still smoking?" Johnny asked. Lee tossed the cigarette butt out into the same spot he threw all of his cigarette butts. He liked to keep them in one spot. It was easier to pick them all up, before he went back home to Lake Charles. Lee was a bachelor, set in his ways.

"Yeah, but I'm quitting after the Song Writers Festival," Lee said. Johnny walked up and shook Lee's sweaty hand. Lee was still grinning. Johnny and he didn't get to visit very often, but they had been friends since childhood.

"Didn't you say you were quitting last year after the Song Writers Festival?" Johnny asked. Lee laughed at the question, put the lawn mower back in the shed, and followed Johnny into the trailer.

"Hey Johnny, you want to go to the Florabama Bar and Grill tonight?" Lee yelled down the hall. Johnny sat his travel bag down in the back bedroom and turned on the air conditioner, hoping to circulate some fresh air. Walking back down the hall to the kitchen, he pondered Lee's question.

"Yeah, whatever you want to do," Johnny said. "I have two weeks off, just getting away from work is enough fun for me." They walked back out to the porch. Lee sat in the lawn chair and lit up another cigarette, Johnny sat in the patio chair next to Lee and took a deep breath. He let it out slowly through clinched teeth. The two of them passed on gossip and rumors of people they both knew, while the stifling heat slowly grew bearable in the sweltering late southern afternoon.

"Come on, JT, let's get some groceries," Lee said. "I'm almost out of cigarettes." Johnny opened one eye and nodded agreement.

"How long have I been asleep?" Johnny asked.

"Not long, ten minutes," Lee said. Johnny slowly climbed off the porch and into Lee's passenger seat. The smoky gray-colored car squealed out into the street on a joy ride to the beach. First things first they checked out the beach conditions and sunbathers, before the supermarket. Patrolling the beachfront for swimmers in danger and girls in interesting swimsuits during the summers, they had both been lifeguards in the summers between college semesters. Beaches still pulled at them like magnets. They shopped through the supermarket aisles, bought some food for breakfast, a six pack of beer, a couple of bottles of red wine, and headed back to the trailer.

Lee's trailer was an old fishing camp that Lee had been borrowing from a friend's father for many years. Finally, a few years back, the owner had decided to sell it and offered it to Lee. Nothing much more than a flophouse, clean and well organized, the lot it sat on was more valuable than the trailer.

Johnny told Lee to wake him up around dark if he wanted to go out, poured himself a glass of wine and went off to his room to take a much-needed nap. Four weeks of working night shift had really screwed up his body clock, he wanted to sleep all day and stay up all night, he was not hungry, didn't feel like talking to anyone, and he couldn't concentrate, but he did feel like sleeping. He turned on the small television set sitting on the dresser in his room as he passed by. Ricky and Lucy were fighting, then hugging, few things never changed. He draped his shirt over the only chair in the room and hooked his pants on the brass clothes hook next to the door. The sheets on the bed were clean and cool as he slipped his aching body between them. Laying his head on the soft pillow he'd caught the sent of a woman's perfume on the pillowcase and his mind slipped off into thoughts of who might have lay on the pillow, while the hum of the window air conditioner slowly lulled him into a deep sleep.

Lee woke up Johnny shortly after dark. Johnny took a shower then grabbed another glass of wine and headed out to the porch where Lee was still smoking cigarettes. Johnny sat next to him and looked out at the stars in the clear night sky. He could smell the salty gulf, a block away.

"I am so tired of going to work and going home, something's got to change," Johnny said. Lee took another long drag from his nearly finished cigarette, and slowly exhaled. Smoke rings fluttered, like birds escaping into the still evening air.

"JT, what you need is a girlfriend, someone to share your life with. You live like a damn hermit," Lee said. Johnny nodded his head in agreement. Talk was easy.

"You're right, I've always been too slow at making new friends," Johnny replied. "And too damn picky when it comes to women." They both laughed.

"But it's worse than that," Johnny said. "I really believe I've squandered my life, at least up to this point."

"JT, you always did tend to moralize too much, you worry too much," Lee said. "Why can't you just enjoy your life? Marry someone, raise a family." Johnny twisted in his chair trying to find a comfortable position. Lee watched him squirm, chuckling out loud.

"I'm not cut out for marriage," Johnny said. "Besides, I'm too old to make a good father now."

"Bullshit, JT," Lee said. "My Grandfather, back in Ireland, got married for the first time at age 66, to a fourteen-year-old and raised six children." Johnny turned to face Lee with a smile on his worried face. Lee made eye contact, bracing himself for the impending insult. His pay back due for telling Johnny to get married when he had never had the courage.

"Lee, I'm glad you told me that," Johnny said. "Now I feel like I know you a little better."

"Hey, screw you," Lee said. Johnny roared with laughter while Lee stood up, tossed his cigarette, and went inside the trailer. As the door slammed, Johnny leaned forward and picked up one of the neighborhood cats that had been hovering around the porch all day. There was an odd thing about cats and Lee, he seemed to have a special communication thing going on with cats. Johnny was sure they just responded to Lee because they could tell he especially enjoyed their company. He had noticed the same behavior around Lee with women.

Johnny and Lee rode out to the Florabama in Johnny's car. Lee told him he was afraid some drunk in the parking lot would scratch his Porsche. Johnny didn't mind driving, he was used to Lee's idiosyncrasies.

Two smiling women working the front door at the Florabama asked for a five-dollar cover charge. Johnny and Lee showed their membership cards and walked past into the recording area of the bar, which was so packed they had to walk sideways through the crowd. Just as they approached the bar counter a man stood up and walked out the door. Lee climbed onto the empty stool, announcing his intention to sit there for a while.

Johnny ordered a glass of red wine from a passing server and told Lee he was going to have a look around. Lee said he would stay on the stool for a while and to let him know if he found anything interesting. Johnny laughed at Lee's one-track mind and gave the server a dollar tip when she brought him a small bottle of wine. He sipped it straight out of the tiny neck of the bottle, and its dry, tart, full body bite, slid down his throat, warming his stomach, numbing him slightly to the noise and bedlam.

"My name's Johnny," he told her. "Most people call me JT." She smiled at him and told him thanks. He looked around the room trying to figure out where he would go first, deciding to start with the pool room. He slipped past a group of locals at the door, still in shock at the crowd of people.

A long haired smiling bouncer wearing a Hawaiian shirt, surfer shorts, flip flop beach sandals, and a beard said hello to Johnny as he walked past. So many people were standing around, there was hardly enough room for the players to position the cue sticks. People politely moved aside every time the players changed positions, like some strange dance, that everyone knew the score to. Johnny jockeyed around the pool tables, smiling to a couple of familiar faces as he looked around the room. He paused a few minutes to visit with a cute young couple from Washington, D.C. while they waited for a turn at the pool table.

Tourists and locals from up and down the beach gathered to sip beer and shoot the bull. Johnny studied the photographs on the wall before, eventually, leaving the poolroom, photos of posing celebrities of the day, on deep sea fishing trips, and vacationers, all obviously working much too hard at relaxing away from the daily grind. Johnny felt compassion for their forced smiles. He wasn't feeling very festive either, try as he might.

He walked up to the lottery sales booth and stopped, waiting for the attendant to hand a tiny woman a ticket. Sticking his right hand into his pocket, he pulled out his money clip and slipped one dollar off the top of the folded bills, laying it on the counter.

"May I have a quick pick on the Florida lottery, please Ma-am?" he asked. The lottery person smiled at him, pressed a few buttons on the machine, and handed over the ticket.

"The Biggest jackpot ever tonight," she said. Johnny could tell she was sincerely excited about her job.

"No kidding," Johnny said. "How much is it?"

"Eighty-two million!" she said. "What could you do with that?" His eyes glazed over as he pondered her question.

"I hate to guess," he finally said. "But I'm fairly confident that it would change my life." They were smiling at each other as their imaginations danced. Johnny thanked her and slipped the ticket into the small change pocket on the right side of his blue jeans.

As he headed outside toward the upstairs bar, he spotted an interesting looking woman with a sad face. She was standing near the top of the wooden stairs leading to the observation deck, staring out into the crowd of people. She had the look of a lost child, but still calmness engulfed her. He studied her as he climbed the stairs heading in her direction. She appeared not to notice him staring at her, even as he stood on the step beside her. As he paused she slowly turned her head to see who was standing there.

"Choctaw?" Johnny asked. He gazed calmly into her dark brown eyes, wondering what her reply would be if she answered at all.

"No, Creek Tribe," she said and peered into his dark brown eyes, unblinking. Eventually her face began a slow genuine smile. Johnny was hypnotized.

"Most people would have thought me rude to walk up to them without an introduction, look them in the eye, face to face, and assume they're American Indian," he said.

"Virginia," she said.

"What?" he asked.

"My name is Virginia," she said again.

"My name is Johnny, but most people call me JT," he said.

They talked for a while sizing each other up, height, build, grace, confidence, intelligence, culture, education, social status, marital status. Then he asked her his favorite question.

"If you could be anybody, anywhere in the world and if social status, education, or money were not factors, who would you be, where would you be, and what would you be doing?" Johnny asked.

He considered this question the quickest way to find out how far along life's journey a person had traveled. The average person usually said something along the lines of, "I'd like to be rich or famous."

Rich and famous, it appeared to Johnny, replaced the traditional American middle class dream of owning a home, raising a family or having your own business.

In days when America was young, and nearly everyone was a newly arrived immigrant, people wanted to own their own property and to have religious freedom. To live in a democracy where the government represented the people's interest, not a king or dictator.

However, the America of modern times had become a place where just getting a job to support a family could be outside the reach of the middle and the lower rungs of society. Even with college degrees, a working husband and wife would often struggle to put food on the table and get their children a decent education. In addition, modern America was one of the wealthiest countries on earth.

Virginia glanced out at the crowd of people down below the stairs. People were standing, dancing, or watching the band play.

"I know that I am here on this earth to be of service to humanity in someway," she said.

"That's the best answer I've ever heard," he said. "Usually after wanting to be rich and famous, I hear things like a professional career."

"What would you do?" she asked. Hardly anyone had returned the question to him over the years.

"I also would serve humanity, somehow," he said.

"Wow, a socially conscious person," she laughed.

"You're not the average Saturday night Florabamian either," he said.

He eventually talked himself out. Usually he didn't talk much, but she had coaxed him along, understanding his point of view on most things. Johnny liked this woman. She intrigued him. But as usual, he excused himself anyway, promising to return and visit with her later, if she were still there. When he met a woman, he was attracted to, he would often get strong urges to hold or kiss her long before his affections could be socially justifiable. Moving away from the woman was Johnny's way of regrouping. Virginia had explained that she was watching for her cousin, who was coming in from out of town and she would be there until she came. Johnny turned and walked away. Her eyes followed him as he moved down the weathered wooden stairs.

Virginia was interesting to Johnny, although younger than the usual female who attracted him. She was close enough to his age, slightly cautious, with a high degree of self-confidence and grace. They were compatible enough, at first glance, he thought to himself.

Johnny wanted a woman in his life. He occasionally got involved in a relationship, but eventually they would give him the ultimatum, "get married or else." He had always chosen the "or else." He didn't understand why marriage was so important to women. As far as he was concerned, marriage was for raising children. He felt he had waited too long now to have children. He considered his child rearing years over.

"It's ten o'clock," the bartender said. "Watch the TV screen up there. They'll show you the winning lottery numbers." Johnny had asked the bartender to let him know when the lottery pull would be televised. Six people were simultaneously flapping their arms trying to get the bartender's attention to order drinks as Johnny thanked him. Johnny felt the cool, humid gulf breeze blowing through his loose shirt as he watched the crowd. Their reverberating noise engulfed him as they yelled to be heard.

An overhead television was broadcasting LSU kicking Florida's butt. Nearly everyone at the Florabama had an opinion about the event one way or the other. A group of women from Louisiana held purple and gold cheerleader pom poms and ran through the crowd cheering every time LSU made a good play.

Susan, a computer programmer, and her boy friend from Washington, D.C., whom Johnny had talked with by the pool tables, were heading toward him. It must be time for them to leave, Johnny thought. She walked up to him, her boy friend following behind.

"Hey, JT, Robert and I are going to leave now," she said. "We wanted you to know we enjoyed the conversation, and to call us if you ever make it to D. C., I'm in the book." She was beaming a beautiful, confident smile so strongly, Johnny thought he might propose to her, right in front of her fiancee.

"If I were you, I would give up trying to get Robert to marry you," Johnny said. "Seven years is a long time, even if he is a physician. You'll have no problem finding a quality guy." Susan leaned into him, slipping her business card into his hand and whispered.

"Thanks, JT, I believe you're right. Goodnight," she said in her husky voice. She gave him a wink as she turned to leave.

"Goodnight," Johnny said out loud. He watched her float down the stairs like an angel on a wing. Johnny waved to her boyfriend and was thinking, "That guy's a fool. Women like that are rare. I wished a girl like that loved me." Johnny took a deep breath and looked back over toward the bar.

"Hey, Bartender," Johnny said. "I didn't get a chance to see those numbers. Did you see the lottery pull?" The bartender checked his note pad by the cash register.

"Yeah—-4,7,12,24,37, and 41-or something like that," he said.

Johnny pulled out his ticket 4,7,12,24,37,41 stared up at him, off the face of the ticket.

"Look at my ticket!" Johnny yelled back over the roar of the gulf and the crowd. The bartender looked at Johnny and laughed.

"I guess you are a winner," he said. Johnny didn't answer him. "Well don't forget you owe me half the money, for sharing those numbers."

"Did I really win?" Johnny's mind raced. "God, don't let me misplace this ticket." Johnny looked over at the rolling surf pounding on the beach down below. His imagination ran wild with possibilities. Of course, that was always the reason he bought tickets anyway. For the few hours or days he held the ticket he could fantasize about what he would do, if he really did win the money.

Johnny's mind slowly floated back into his body, and he looked at the crowd around him enjoying the cool night air. It amazed him how people could enjoy themselves at the drop of a hat. Carefully, he stuffed the lottery ticket back into his change pocket.

"I gotta check these numbers out. I'll see you later," Johnny said. He tossed two dollars on the bar. The bartender didn't glance up.

"Somebody pinch me! I've got to be dreaming!" Johnny kept thinking. "God in heaven, please get me to the lady in the lottery ticket booth." He maneuvered his way around a drunk, grossly overweight, bald-headed man who had been boring a young couple so badly they left just to get away from him.

Johnny's heart raced in his chest, his face glowed red, and he bumped into people like a drunken person. He felt as though he were running for a slow motion touch down. As he reached the lottery ticket sales booth, the crowd around him roared with excitement. He wondered if they had been watching his struggle, but LSU had scored again. He maneuvered to a place in the crooked ticket line. People pushed and shoved squeezing between him and the girl in front of him, apparently trying to get to the restrooms. A guy ahead of him told a joke to his blond date.

"What do you call four cars, with four blond drivers, at a four-way stop?" the guy said. His blond date gave him an evil look.

"What?" she asked.

"Eternity!" he screamed out with drunkened laughter. Johnny cringed at the insult. The woman saw no humor in his verbal abuse and slugged him. Johnny chuckled quietly to himself.

At last, it was his turn to advance to the booth. He pulled his lottery ticket from his change pocket to make sure he didn't get the numbers wrong. His fingers felt weak and his palms so sweaty he dropped the ticket on the floor. He quickly recovered his lost treasure and stood up to face the woman working the booth. She smiled at him.

"Miss-pardon me," Johnny said to the fourtyish girl working the booth. She smiled again. Johnny was six feet tall, with classically hand-some features he'd inherited from his mostly French ancestry. He had a broad smile covered by a too long black mustache. He usually kept his dark brown hair average length, but like tonight, he didn't comb it or cut it often enough.

"Yes, Sir?" she answered.

"Miss, could you double check these numbers," Johnny said. He slowly read off the numbers from the lottery ticket in his hands. "4,7,12,24,37, and 41. I uh-my friend thinks they might have the winning ticket for tonight's lottery," Johnny said.

"I can't tell you if those are the correct numbers. Where is your friend?" she asked. She looked at Johnny with an unbelieving smile. Johnny stared back with a dumbfounded look. "The machine won't show the numbers until after midnight."

"Oh, uh, he's watching the band, I'll go tell him," Johnny said. He wondered if she believed him. He hated lying.

"Don't forget me when you collect the money," she told him. His feeling of elation rapidly turned to deflation as he moved away from the ticket counter. Johnny turned, looking around to see if anyone had been listening. No one appeared to have heard him try to confirm the numbers. He tucked the lottery ticket back into the money clip and put it back into his right front blue-jean pocket. The waitress passed in front of Johnny again.

"Hey, waitress, remind me to buy you a new car," Johnny said to her.

"You're crazy," the waitress said and smiled as she began serving a nearby table. She glanced back over the table at Johnny as he squeezed by. "But if you don't mind, make it a convertible." Johnny laughed at her audacity.

"I gotta get out of here," Johnny thought then remembered Virginia and wondered if she was still at the top of the stairs. He had told her he would be back to visit before he left, and he wanted to leave now.

Johnny stepped to the outside area but didn't see her anywhere. She had to be around somewhere, he thought. Scanning the gyrating crowd, he finally saw her standing like a female wooden Indian with a slight smile on her face, as she talked to her newly arrived cousin.

Virginia's husband Michael had told her when they first met that she looked as if she had come straight off an Indian reservation, and Virginia had told him, she had no idea how much American Indian blood ran through her veins.

As soon as Johnny took a step in Virginia's direction, her eyes locked onto him. She watched him as though she could read his mind, as if he wore his thoughts written on his forehead. As he walked over to her she slowly turned to face him.

"Hey, Virginia, I really enjoyed talking," Johnny said. "I like to know more about the Sweat Lodges you attended and the White Buffalo Calf that was born. Do you really believe that Indian legend, that says the White Buffalo Calf being born announces the beginning of a thousand years of no evil?"

"Yes, I am sure of it!" Virginia said. Her look changed to dead serious. Johnny was interested in American Indian religious beliefs. He also had a small amount of Indian blood in his veins.

"Would you mind if I called you?" Johnny said. He felt uncomfortable asking her if he could call her. After all, she was married. Johnny told himself his intentions were friendly, common interests.

"No, I wouldn't mind if you called," Virginia said. "My last name is Forest, I live in Foley, and I'm in the phone book." She had a very knowing look. When they talked, Johnny felt they already knew what the other was going to say before it was said.

Johnny looked at her, wondering if his hair was messed up. He was trying to end the conversation quickly but not too abruptly. Finding his buddy Lee was his next goal and then to see if Lee needed a ride home.

"I really would like to talk more about your horses too," Johnny said. "You seem to know more about horses than anyone I've ever met." His father had given him a horse when he was young and he'd always hoped to get another one some day.

"Yeah, you should come by and ride with us," Johnny heard Virginia saying. But his mind was thinking about leaving as he began to experience a panic attack. In the past year, he had been getting them often, and he wondered if the attacks were caused by repeated exposure to the nerve gases at work.

"Uh, Virginia if you don't mind," Johnny said. "I'll give you a call in a few weeks when I come in for the Song Writers Festival."

"All right. See you later," she said. She was smiling at Johnny like he was a little schoolboy. He turned to walk away from her thinking, "If I were ever to get rich, I wouldn't be able to trust anyone's motives. I wouldn't know who my real friends were."

"Jeez, what a dreamer I am," he said out loud. "Winning the lottery would be like being given the key to a dream machine." Dream machine. Johnny liked the sound of that.

Johnny thought another glass of wine might calm his nerves and asked the waitress for a glass as she brushed past him again. He followed her to the waitress station at the bar, gave her five bucks, and told her to keep the change. Sipping it, he looked for Lee in the flowing mass of people. Lee had been in the recording area watching the musicians play the last time Johnny had seen him. Maybe he was still there.

Walking through the doorway Johnny realized a woman musician was playing Mary-Chapin Carpenter's "I Feel Lucky Tonight," about winning the lottery, Johnny thought again that there are no coincidences in life as he slowly maneuvered his way through the crowd, being careful not to touch the oversize garbage can or to push anyone. Across the room, he could see a throng of women giggling around Lee, who was still sitting on the same stool near the entrance.

Johnny could never figure out how Lee did it, but women and cats flocked to him everywhere he went. Lee had told Johnny it was a curse. Johnny had told Lee, "Throw me in that briar patch."

"Lee," Johnny broke through the group, "I hate to interrupt y'all. Please forgive me, I'll just take a second of your time."

"Hey JT, what's wrong?" Lee said with a puzzled look on his face.

"Lee, I've got to get out of here," Johnny told him.

"What are you talking about JT?" Lee asked. "We just got here an hour and a half ago."

"Lee, I can't tell you in here," Johnny said. "If you want to get a ride home with someone or take a taxi, I'll see you at the trailer-but I'm going home."

"Hold on, JT, I'm coming," Lee said. "I don't think I've ever seen you this anxious to leave, What's going on?"

"You probably won't believe me," Johnny said. "but, I think I've won the lottery!" Lee turned to face Johnny. Johnny didn't really believe he'd won the lottery, but he didn't want to say I'm having a panic attack either.

"Right, JT, show me the ticket," Lee laughed.

"I'm telling you, Lee, I won-when we get in the car, I'll show you the winning ticket," Johnny said. "I don't want to take a chance of losing it in here."

"JT, you serious?" Lee said. "Look, can I have a 10% share, if you've really won?" Lee had a serious look on his face.

"Lee, we've been through this already today in the supermarket," Johnny said. "I told you if you would buy a lottery ticket too, and either of us wins, we'll split 50/50. And you said, no, you were going to save your dollar."

Lee turned away, ignoring Johnny.

Lee didn't truly believe Johnny could have the winning ticket, but he wasn't a 100% sure he didn't either. Johnny was known to pull an occasional practical joke, but this was bigger than the usual charade he had pulled in the past.

"Just think, one little dollar this afternoon," Johnny said. "And you'd own half of the largest lottery jackpot ever to be given away in the State of Florida." The women surrounding Lee were catching bits and pieces of the conversation between the two men. They didn't know if Johnny was joking either, but they were edging very close to him, smiling and giggling at everything he said.

"You're bullshitting me, JT," Lee said. "Show me the damn ticket." Lee got up and followed Johnny out the front door into the cool night air. Johnny just ignored Lee, thinking he might be wealthy now and already he was having trouble with his friends.

"No, I don't think I will, Lee," Johnny said. He dodged a group of tourist heading for the entry, then turned and headed toward the parking lot. As the two men crossed the crushed oyster shell main front parking lot, a group of Harley Davidson motorcycle riders roared in and put down their kickstands.

Bike riders could generally be divided into three groups, Johnny believed. American bike riders, Japanese bike riders, and German bike riders. Harley Davidson riders down South tended to be good ole boys, in bad boy wardrobes. They were a different breed from the other motorcycle enthusiasts. Japanese bike riders native to the Gulf Coast wore any kind of work or street clothes, including shorts and flip-flops. BMW riders rode with bullet proof Gore-Tex looking zoot suits, stronger than leather with high top European-styled riding boots. They looked as though they might have just climbed off a horse after some high tech English foxhunt.

"Hey, JT," one of the Harley riders yelled. "Is it crowded in there?" Lee turned to see who was calling out to Johnny.

"Who the hell are they, JT?" Lee asked. The rest of the riders were getting off their bikes and taking off their helmets.

"Some guys I work with," Johnny said. "They went through mid-life crises and came out with motorcycles. I guess that's better than a divorce." Two of the gnarly looking black leather jacket clad riders walked over to Johnny.

"Hey, JT, is it crowded in there?" A rider named Rocco asked. Lee stepped around to the other side of Johnny.

"Didn't mean to scare y'all?" Rocco said smiling at Lee. Lee smiled back, slightly embarrassed.

Johnny dug in his pocket for his car keys as Pim, the second rider, unzipped his jacket and put his bike key in a pocket.

"Yeah, the place is full of tourists," Johnny said. "Some of them are nice looking, too. Where are the wives?" Rocco gave a quick wink as he put his bike keys into his pants pocket.

"At home I guess," Pim laughed.

"Hey, JT," Pim said. "Rocco and I are going to ride out West in May. You still got your bike?"

"Yeah, Pim," Johnny said. "I don't ride it very often, but it still looks and works like new. Where out West are y'all going?"

"Taos, New Mexico," Pim said. "And maybe to some cliff dwellings in southern Colorado. You want to come along?" Johnny smiled at the idea.

"Wow, that's a coincidence," Johnny said. "I was just talking to a woman in there about a Pueblo in Taos. When are y'all leaving?" Johnny was looking at Pim but his mind was thinking about getting to sleep.

"First half of May," Pim said. "Let's get together soon to talk." Johnny agreed they all would talk about it when they got back to work.

"It's a small world, isn't it?" Johnny said as they headed to the car. Lee was still thinking about the possibility that Johnny might really have won the lottery.

"JT, level with me," Lee said. "Why are we leaving, What did you do, piss off some woman's boyfriend or something?" Johnny laughed out loud at Lee's suggestion.

"No, Lee, not tonight, at least not yet," he grinned. Lee shook his head and climbed in Johnny's car. Johnny was so tired his clutch leg trembled as he tried to find reverse.

BIG EASY, CENTER OF THE SOUTHERN GULF COAST

Driving out to Bear Point, Johnny and Lee talked about taking another trip down into Copper Canyon, Mexico. They had gone there last spring and it had unexpectedly turned out to be an even greater adventure than they hoped.

Copper Canyon, in the northern Mexico Sierras, was four times larger than the Grand Canyon in the United States. There are train robbers and isolated Indian tribes still living in caves without modern conveniences. Observing the aboriginal people living isolated lives in the Sierra summits had opened Johnny's eyes to the excessive, self-absorbed life styles many Americans live.

Middle class America's basic living standards were unattainable for most of the world. Air conditioning, television, multiple automobiles, fast food joints, drug stores, and bank accounts were far from the average indigenous Mexican people's lives. About as likely as a middle class American becoming the King or Queen of England.

"Hey, JT, you want to stop at the Keg and get a pizza?" Lee asked. "I'm starving."

"No way, Lee," Johnny said. "I can't eat right now, my body is too messed up from a month of working nights. I just need to climb into bed to sleep for a couple of days. I'll drop myself by the trailer, you can go back to the Keg with my car."

"Okay Mr. Lottery Winner," Lee said. "No appetite, huh? Hell you should be in there buying pizza for the whole place." Johnny drove down the road smiling to himself. He didn't really believe he'd won the lottery, the bartender certainly had written down the wrong numbers. But it had been a lot of fun watching Lee squirming over thinking he did.

"Tell me, Johnny, what are you going to do with all the money?" Lee asked. A car from behind suddenly swerved around them, flashing its lights and blowing its horn. As it sped out in front Johnny checked his speed and made an adjustment on his speed control.

"I don't have the money yet," Johnny said. He was hoping Lee would forget about the lottery money. What was meant to be only a joke was getting out of hand.

"I can't believe you're not going to give me some of the money if you've really won?" Lee said. Johnny checked his speedometer again and looked in the rear view mirror.

"Lee, now don't let my being rich change our friendship," Johnny said. He was uncomfortable discussing the probably fictitious win, but watching Lee worry over it was a lot of fun. Even if he really had won he wouldn't feel the money was his just to spend any way he desired.

"Hell, we've been friends most of our lives," Lee said. "We made it through puberty and lately early middle age. At our age I'd say our friendship has weathered a few storms."

"Yeah, you're right," Johnny smiled.

"What are you going to do with all the power, JT?" Lee persisted. Johnny adjusted his seat back and rechecked his speed. That was an 82-million-dollar question. That kind of money could be a dream machine and Johnny was going to dream a while.

"I really don't have a clue," Johnny said. "I guess it would be wise to think about it for a while, but first I've got to see if I really won. Then I guess I should set up some kind of corporation to hold the money for me. I read a story in Reader's Digest about someone who won. He waited fifty-one weeks to collect. But before that I would think about it a few months, before I collected the money. I guess then I'd be a little closer to a plan of distribution."

"Distribution," Lee said. "Look, JT, when you start distributing don't forget me." He was looking at Johnny wide-eyed!

"Lee, you are just so damned persistent, I believe I would have a position for you, in my new corporation," Johnny laughed.

"What corporation, JT," Lee asked. "What are you talking about?" Johnny smiled back at him.

"I can't tell you much about Dream Machine, Inc. right now," Johnny said. "But if I really did win, I'd have a need for a person with your persistent talents."

"JT, I don't come cheap," Lee countered. Johnny put his blinker on and took a left turn into the Bear Point Marina subdivision.

"Lee, I got a feeling if I picked up your living expenses-and paid you a salary you'd follow anywhere, anywhere that interested you, I should say," Johnny grinned.

"JT, it sounds interesting, so far," Lee said. "But we'll discuss it later when you really collect the money. In the meantime leave me your car keys, I'm going to get something to eat." Johnny pulled into the driveway, stopped and climbed out, while Lee walked around the car and slid into the driver's seat.

"I'll see you in the morning," Johnny said. As he turned and walked toward the porch, Lee backed out onto South Pensacola Drive.

In the back bedroom Johnny took off his smoky-smelling clothes, threw them onto the floor in the closet, and took a steaming hot shower. Toweling off, he turned on the TV, adjusted the sleep-timer for off in half an hour, then pulled the shades tight. The next morning he didn't think about watching TV or buying a lottery ticket until he had run a wash and was folding his blue jeans.

His towel from last night was still damp hanging on the doorknob. Taking his jeans out of the dryer, he dug in the change pocket. No ticket. Just pieces of paper fragments mingled with the warm clothes. Sunlight was peeking through the bent mini blind shades in the bedroom sending sparkling beams of light filled with tiny floating specs of dust into the dark hall where Johnny folded his clothes leaning against the dark wood-paneled wall.

"Damn it, I don't even remember the numbers now," Johnny said. "I'll never know if I won or not." He couldn't believe his luck. Forgetting a possible winning lottery ticket in his pants pocket, that had to be the peak of stupidity, he told himself. He blamed it on shift work. His body clock kept him confused half the time. That afternoon he and Lee worked around the trailer cleaning and repairing. Neither spoke about the lottery ticket. Johnny refused to talk about it, and Lee had come to seriously doubt Johnny had really won.

Monday morning Johnny loaded up his car while Lee cooked breakfast. They said their usual good-byes, did their usual handshakes, and Johnny headed back out to Madisonville. Four hours on the road and he arrived back at his boat, fixed himself a bowl of cereal, grabbed Walter Russell's book, "World Crisis," and stayed in bed reading the rest of the day.

<p style="text-align:center">~~~</p>

Tuesday morning Johnny used the marina pay phone to call the 1-900 number of the Florida State Lottery tickets, trying to verify from memory that his ticket might have been the winning ticket. The automated voice on the telephone said:

"If you would like to hear winning lottery numbers press 1

-If you would like to hear the winning lottery numbers for the month of October press 2

-If you would like to hear the winning lottery numbers for the month of September press 3

-If you know the extension of the person you are trying to reach please enter the extension now

-If you don't have a touch-tone telephone please hold for an operator," the telephone robotically commanded. Johnny held the line for what seemed like ten minutes.

"Hello this is the Florida State Lottery Corporation, may I help you?" a live human voice finally spoke.

"Yes, Ma'am," Johnny said. "I believe my friend has the winning lottery ticket for last Saturday night. Could you please confirm the numbers?"

"Sir," the voice said. "If you or your friend wants to check the winning lottery numbers, I'll connect you to the recording that gives that information."

"No Ma'am," Johnny said. "I don't really want to check the winning numbers, just please tell me how long do I-I mean, how long does my friend have before they have to collect on this past Saturday's lottery."

"What's your question, sir?" she asked.

"The 82 million dollar jackpot lottery from last Saturday night," Johnny gasped. "How long does my friend have to bring the ticket in and collect the money before the ticket expires?"

"Oh, I see-sir, what is your friend's name?" she asked. Johnny wondered if he should give her his real name or a fake name.

"Uh, no Ma'am I can't say," Johnny said. "Just yet. But please tell me how long do we have to collect the money and what's the method and location for collecting the jackpot?" The operator gave an audible sigh of frustration.

"Sir, for last weeks 82 million-dollar lottery, the collection deadline is exactly one year to the date from when the lottery was pulled," she said. Johnny gave an audible sigh of relief.

"And what's the method and location Ma'am?" Johnny added. All this conversation about 82 million dollars was starting to raise Johnny's blood pressure. He could hear his heart beating in his ears.

"Oh, yes, sir," she said. "I'm sorry. The location is in Jacksonville, Florida. You'll have to bring the winning ticket and sign documents.

Then we'll cut a check for the value of the annuity after taxes or you can collect the annuity monthly over a twenty-year period."

"Miss, what is the amount after taxes?" Johnny asked. He didn't like asking all these questions from an obviously uninterested woman, but he had a right to know the answers.

"Sir, I can't give that information over the phone," she said. "But if you'd give me your friend's name, I'll make an appointment for her," she said. Johnny wondered if he said something to cause the lottery receptionist to think his make-believe friend was a woman.

"Uh, no Ma'am," Johnny said. "My friend is a guy and, uh, I can't give you his name right now, but, uh, he'll give you a call soon." He didn't want the receptionist to tell the public that a woman had won the lottery and then have a guy show up with the winning ticket.

"Sir," the voice said. "The numbers are 4,7,12,24,37,41." Those numbers rang through Johnny's mind. He was certain those were the numbers, he had once owned.

"Thank you," Johnny said. He hung up the telephone and sat thinking in the chair outside the marina pay phone. Johnny believed this lottery business was real now. He knew exactly how long he had to work out the problem of being rich, if he could find the ticket, if he hadn't washed it. He walked back out to his car, looked under all the seats and in the glove box. He found several old Louisiana lottery tickets that he had never checked and shoved them into his pocket to deal with later. Johnny sat in the driver's seat of his car, begging God to return the ticket to him.

"God, if you'll help me find my ticket, I promise to rededicate my life and all the money I get to trying to make the world a better place," Johnny prayed. Figuring out good ways to use it would mean hard work and a lot of trouble, Johnny knew. If he ever collected 82 million dollars his life would never be the same. Everyone who even remotely knew him would probably treat him differently. That worried Johnny.

People would begin asking him for favors even complete strangers would be calling his house. Johnny thought. Then he remembered he didn't own a telephone. Well, they might come to his boat, he warned himself. Johnny was already having a hard time being rich and he didn't have the ticket nor the money as of yet, and likely never would.

Johnny got a beep from Lee on his pager, so he returned Lee's call while he was near the marina telephone.

"Hey, JT," Lee said. "Did you ever get in touch with the lottery people?" Lee asked immediately. Johnny wished he'd never told Lee about the damn ticket.

"Yeah, Lee," Johnny said. "Sure did, but I really won't believe it till I get the money in my hand." Johnny was trying to change the subject without letting on he did, indeed, without a doubt, for sure, used to, have the winning ticket. But he knew he wouldn't be able to keep it a secret from Lee. Eventually it would come out.

"JT, I haven't mentioned you winning the lottery to anyone, just like you asked me," Lee said. "But the Monday Orange Beach newspaper said the winning lottery ticket was sold from the Florabama Saturday night. They said it was a quick pick. Was the ticket you bought a quick pick or did you choose the numbers?"

"That's right, Lee," Johnny said. "My ticket was a quick pick, and it had all the right numbers."

"JT, what are you waiting on," Lee said. "I'd be collecting today if I won. You are liable to lose the damn thing if you're not careful. Besides I'm dying to tell people about this."

"Look, Lee," Johnny said. "I've got one year from last Saturday. That gives me time to check into taxes and other things. But while I'm doing that don't tell a soul, please."

"Taxes? why in the world would you worry about taxes?" Lee wanted to know. "Even if they take half the money, you still got more than forty million dollars!" The telephone was silent for a few seconds.

"Yeah, and lost forty million," Johnny explained. "I prefer to at least make a little effort to save forty million dollars." The telephone was silent again.

"Look I've got to go," Lee said. "I'll call you soon."

"Lee, before you go," Johnny said, "Do you know any tax lawyers?" He thought if he ever got to collect the money it would be smart to set up a corporation.

"No, JT," Lee said. "You might check with Andy and see what he says." Johnny had forgotten about Andrew's being a lawyer. But if he remembered correctly, Andrew defended insurance companies only.

Johnny hung up the telephone with Lee and looked up Andrew's telephone number. Wanda, the harbor master walked by waving to Johnny as she went up the stairs to her office. Johnny carefully dialed his calling card number into the telephone and then entered Andrew's number. The law firm's young receptionist answered the telephone with her happy youthful voice. When Johnny asked to speak with Andrew, she said she wasn't sure he was in but she would ring his office. Andrew answered the telephone with his usual jovial voice.

"Hello, Andrew, this is JT. How's your family doing?" Johnny asked. Andrew was hard to catch up with both at home and at the office. Johnny was fortunate to have caught him on his first try.

"Everyone's doing fine, Johnny. How's everything with you?" he asked.

"Fine, Andrew. Are you coming to the Song Writers Festival in November?" Johnny added.

"No, I'm too busy this year, Johnny," he replied. "But I really wanted to go this year."

"Andrew, I might need some help with income tax laws," Johnny said. He should have visited longer before he asked Andrew for help, but all Johnny could think about was the lottery money, right now.

"It's a little early for tax season, Johnny," Andrew countered. "The IRS call you in for an audit or anything?"

"No. I could be getting a lump sum of money sometime in the next year and I have some tax questions," Johnny said. He was hoping Andrew didn't ask too many more questions.

"Hey, that's great, JT, but you know I don't practice tax law," he said. "I'm still doing insurance defense. However, I can recommend you to a fellow in New Orleans." Johnny's silence encouraged him to go on.

Curtiss DeVedrine 49

"He's an old family friend. His name is Dan Rice," Andrew said, "kind of a spooky looking guy. His office is in the old French Quarter on Royal street, not too far from Pat O'Brien's on Saint Peters."

"All right, I know about where that is," Johnny said.

"He practices inheritance and tax law. If anyone can help you, he can," Andrew said. Johnny's spirits rose. He was only an hour away from Dan Rice's office.

"Andrew, Karen's having a Christmas party this year up in Woodville," Johnny said. "She asked me to invite you."

"Count me in," Andrew replied. "Karen throws the best parties, I still think about the one she threw two years ago. I must have had a blast Melanie was mad at me for weeks afterwards."

"Andrew," Johnny continued. "Lee and I have been going to the Song Writer's Festival for five years now. You'd really enjoy it if you came along." He already knew Andrew wouldn't be coming this year.

"All right, JT, I'll call you next week. Tell Dan Rice I said hello," Andrew closed.

"All right, see you soon," Johnny said. "Tell Melanie and the kids hello for me."

Johnny walked across the marina's white shell parking lot, down the wooden pier to his slip, and climbed aboard his boat. The marina was a quiet place to live. He liked being on the water and often thought about casting his ropes off the dock cleats and going around the world.

It was an ambition he'd held since he was a small child. Johnny's great-uncle Theodore was a career Merchant Marine and would come over to visit once or twice a year when Johnny was a boy. He would fill Johnny's mind with descriptions of distant ports and leave a coin or two from some strange country Johnny had never heard of.

What was Janis Joplin's line from her song? "Freedom's just another word for nothing left to lose." One of the things that Johnny liked about a sailboat was that the finite size limited his instinct to collect at least the big things. He loved to collect antique books and old sailing relics. Johnny loved history. He often wished he had studied to be an

Archeologist or an Anthropologist. The boat limited him to the essentials in life. It was austere, but it kept him from spending most of his time maintaining possessions.

Soon he was having trouble keeping his eyes open and he decided to take a nap. He turned the boat's radio to 88.3 on the FM dial in New Orleans and fell asleep listening to a woman's voice reading the New Orleans Times Picayune newspaper.

His pager beeped, pulling him out of a deep sleep. Trying to figure out if it was day or night, he sat up in bed and grabbed his pants from the brass clothes hook on the bulkhead next to his berth. The number on the beeper belonged to his friend Karen in Woodville, Mississippi. She seldom called him, so he put on his faded blue work shirt, baggy blue jeans and a baseball cap and climbed into his inflatable dinghy. He guessed she wanted to ask him over to visit.

He maneuvered the dinghy out of the marina and across the Tchefuncta River to the Madisonville town dock near a tiny hamburger shop and tied up to a hand rail by the waterfront steps. He knew he should take the time to prepare some healthier food for himself, but this was too much more convenient.

He gave the waitress at the to go window his order as he dug through his pant's pocket for his money clip to pay for his order and count how much money he came home with from Gulf Shores, a lottery ticket slipped from between the folded bills and floated to the ground. Johnny dropped everything he held and dove for the descending ticket.

The girl working the front counter opened the sliding glass window and sat Johnny's food order on the counter. She looked all around wondering if her customer had left without getting his food. Johnny stood up frightening her.

"How much do I owe you?" Johnny asked, then bent down again to finish picking up the lottery ticket, credit cards, money and money clip scattered at his feet. This time she stuck her head out of the window to look down to see what Johnny was doing.

"Four dollars and twenty-eight cents," she said. "Most of my customers stand at the window. I almost didn't see you down there." Johnny reached up and handed her five one-dollar bills, then stood up, thanked her, grabbed the bag and headed for his dinghy. He could hear the girls in the shop giggling as he walked away. Climbing into the dinghy, he unfolded the ticket, hoping and praying audibly. He was afraid it was an old Louisiana lottery ticket, one he had bought a month or so ago. He had a bad habit of not checking his lottery tickets, just letting them collect in his glove box or on the navigation desk in the boat. Eventually, two or three times a year, he threw them away in an effort to straighten up or declutter.

A lottery ticket with the numbers 4,7,12,24,37 and 41 shook in his trembling hand. He checked the date and state. This was it! This was the one! Eighty-two million dollars! Johnny let out a "yahoo" over the waterfront that frightened sea gulls off their perches on the nearby swing bridge. He tucked the ticket carefully back into his money clip and rode the dinghy out to the ancient lighthouse overlooking the lake. Step by step he climbed the spiral staircase to the top of the old tower, carrying his bag of food. This was his private meditation spot, only approachable by water, insulating him like a moat from uninvited human beings. The old lighthouse had been built in that location in 1830's, at a time when most of the American continent was still inhabited primarily by nature. It now served as Johnny's private prayer chapel and only sometimes as an occasional boater's guiding light in trying to find Madisonville in a fog or at night.

In the fading evening light he ate his food and watched the sunset, while dreaming of ways to spend his newly found fortune. A life style consisting of fast cars, big boats, and no more working was dancing in his imagination, the easy life from here on out. Too good to be true, he thought.

A thunderstorm was rolling in from the north, one of those isolated, but forceful fronts that blew through with little or without warning in the hot summer months, a reminder that Mother Nature always reserved the right to rearrange her furniture anytime she saw fit. Johnny had been looking south and west over the lake. The evening sunset changed colors and shapes over the distant New Orleans skyline. Yellows changed to oranges to pinks and reds. He hadn't noticed that darkness had come faster than it should.

The moment he knew he was in trouble it was too late to make a dinghy run for the marina. Johnny had been standing leaning against the top rail of the lighthouse staring out across the lake at the distant sunset. The automated, light-sensitive lighthouse beam had yet to begun its slow motion strobe light evening performance.

Without warning, the world around him flashed brighter and whiter than daylight at high noon as if someone had flashed a giant camera. That flash would forever remain imprinted in his mind. Instinctually, Johnny dove to the floor as the sound of the lightning caught up with the bolt flashing over his head. The hair on his body stood up, from fear or static electricity he didn't know.

Leaping to his feet, he descended the spiral stairs, half-running, half-falling to the bottom. A second bolt of lightning struck the top of the lighthouse. He could hear the spotlight shatter over head as shards of glass rained down over him.

He raced through the low doorway, planning a dash for the dinghy. Waves on the lake were swelling to more than three feet. The dinghy, which Johnny had dragged onto the shore was being blown back out into the lake by the driving rain coming from the north. He ran through the fifty mile-an-hour wind and hammering rain into the lake and dove for the dinghy's bowline as it rapidly slipped away. A few strokes took him along-side the dinghy but the waves were breaking over him making it impossible to climb into the boat. Instead, he swung his limbs frantically and began swimming toward shore with the dinghy rope clinched in his teeth. A rogue wave nearly five feet high flipped the dinghy on top of him smashing his head against the cement breaker rocks in the lighthouse breakwater.

Nearly unconscious, Johnny felt the brackish water stinging the back of his head and he knew he was cut, he hoped not too badly. A second rogue wave slammed the boat on top of him again, pounding his body on the rocks. This time his felt a shooting pain in his back. Large waves sometimes traveled in groups of three, and Johnny wondered how he could survive a third one.

Then he found himself floating above the water. He looked down and could see his limp body floating under the dinghy in the cold dark water. It saddened him to think he may have died, and that it was a shame because his body looked as though it still had plenty of use left in it. He pledged his life to God and asked if he could be spared. He wasn't ready to die. He just needed a breath of air. His mind flashed back to a recent vow, only a few hours ago, when he prayed for the return of a lottery ticket.

He felt land under his feet and mustered all his strength as he shoved the dinghy up, gasping for air. A chill ran down his spine causing him to shiver. Timing the waves he flipped the dinghy upright using the wind at his back as a mechanical advantage. The gray cold water between him and the dinghy swelled, pulling at him, an undertow pulling out to the deep water. He grabbed the bow rope again with renewed strength, and using the waves to surf the boat he pulled it onto shore. With the little strength he had left, he tied the bowline to a small but stout tree and dashed back into the lighthouse entrance. He shivered as he leaned against the wall under the stairs waiting for the storm to die down. He whispered his prayers aloud. The storm ended as suddenly as it had appeared. If it hadn't been for the evidence of his beat up body, he could have imagined the whole thing as a weird dream.

Johnny bailed the muddy water out the dinghy and rinsed the blood off his shoulders, back, and chest. Head wounds always bleed profusely. He rode home on the still slightly choppy lake, the dark, abandoned shore gave him an eerie feeling as though he was being watched. He finally pulled into his slip at the marina at the stern of the Dream Catcher, tied off to the small cleat on the starboard side, and went aboard. Carefully taking everything out of his pants pockets, he laid out his beeper, credit cards, money clip, and the lottery ticket to dry on the boat's galley table. The lottery ticket was wet and wrinkled, but thankfully whole and readable. Johnny sighed while making the Sign of the Cross. His black plastic beeper didn't look as if it had made it through the storm as the small gray LED readout was blank.

After a hot shower he walked back out to the marina pay phone.

"Yes, Karen," he replied. "I understand some of our old high school friends are getting together this weekend, but I've got to work, I'm sorry."

"Haven't you been running down to Gulf Shores with Lee?" she asked him. Only an old friend could question him that way.

"Yes, Karen," he said. "But when my vacation is used up, it's gone. I could take time off without pay, but I can't afford that." He didn't mind visiting with Karen, he just didn't want to spend his vacation time to do it.

"When are you going to come up to visit?" Karen asked. "We'll postpone the get-together until you can make it. Or should we just have it without you?" She was giving up on seeing him. She hadn't seen him in several months, and figured Christmas would come soon enough.

"Oh, I just remembered I need to run into New Orleans in the morning," he said. "I'll call you back tomorrow. I should have a better idea of my schedule by then." He wanted to find out about collecting the lottery money and paying taxes. He figured he might be busy doing that for a while.

Karen was a great friend. She was probably one of the nicest people he knew. He felt bad about how seldom he got to see her. Nevertheless, no matter how hard he tried, he simply didn't have enough time to do everything.

Early morning, the people who lived aboard boats were walking off the docks heading to work. The shell parking lot around the telephone was muddy with rainwater from the night before. Rain had fallen a lot lately. Johnny had heard the weatherman saying it would be a wet winter. He figured it had begun. He picked up the telephone to call Dan Rice's office again.

"Hello, this is Johnny Thumper. I'd like to speak with Mr. Rice," he said politely.

"Do you have an appointment?" the female voice asked.

"No," Johnny replied. He was wondering if he should mention Andrew's name, yet.

"A meeting pertaining to what, Mr. Thumper?" she said.

"I have a tax problem I need help with," Johnny said.

"I'm sorry, sir," she said. "Mr. Rice is not taking any new clients." She sounded as though she was about to hang up.

"Would you tell Mr. Rice that I'm a friend of Andrew Johnson's?" Johnny said. "And that it's very important that I see him soon, if possible."

"Yes Mr. Thumper," she said. "If you'll call back in a few minutes, I'll speak with him."

"Thank you, Ma'am," Johnny replied. He thought his, "Yes Ma'am" sounded a little bit too much like an Elvis Presley impersonator. As he hung up the telephone and walked the fifteen feet into the Crosswinds Café and Bar to order some coffee. As he sipped the steaming brew, he watched the small crowd drink their morning cans of beer or steaming cups of dark roast coffee. The choice of morning beverage depended on who had to go to work and who didn't. Through the large plate glass windows, visible were the neat rows of pleasure boats tied to the floating docks as they danced in unison to the occasional wakes of passing work boats heading down the river toward the Lake Pontchartrain. The morning crowd began to thin out and Johnny stopped daydreaming to phone Dan Rice again hoping for a better response this time. The telephone conversation went a lot smoother.

"Hello, Mr. Thumper, sorry for making you wait," she said. "Mr. Rice said he could see you at eight o'clock tomorrow morning, if you can make it?"

"I'll be there. Thank you very much," Johnny said.

Living on the North Shore of New Orleans was not a bad way to live until you had to go into the city. Then you could count on spending almost a full day on an errand trying to get in and out combating the city traffic. Johnny usually tried to combine business with pleasure when he did drive into the Big Easy.

EVERYONE'S PURSUIT OF HAPPINESS

Thursday Morning

The Causeway traffic across the Lake Pontchartrain was light that morning as Johnny went to meet with Dan Rice. On days with severe weather the Causeway police reduced the traffic to a painful crawl. Then it could take an hour to cross the nearly thirty-mile bridge, the longest bridge in the world when first built.

Johnny pulled out of the marina before sunrise. The waves on the north shore showed only a slight chop, yet, when he neared the south shore the waves had risen up to two-foot swells. The difference in water conditions on the two shores of the same lake always amazed Johnny. He wound his way through the sparse early morning Big Easy traffic, then dropped off the interstate at the Super Dome exit. As he pulled into a parking spot in the French Quarter within a block of where Dan Rices office Johnny checked his watch, 7:40, he had a few minutes to spare.

The sights and smells of the French Quarter in the morning were unique from any other place he had ever seen. He enjoyed strolling down the ancient narrow streets. Each morning the pavement wore a fresh coating of food, litter, alcohol and passed out drunks, all conveniently lying where they were last the night before.

The restaurant supply delivery people rushed back and forth from their vehicles at the curbs. They brought in fresh supplies for the seven-nights-a-week pleasure seekers.

Merchants casually washed down their sidewalks with water hoses, bleach, and soap so their morning patron's shoes wouldn't stick to the pavement. The smell of rotten beer rose from the gutters as the sun warmed the old town.

Early morning dog owners walked their pets before locking them back up in their apartments or tiny back yards on their way out to work.

Overweight, blue-haired, insomniac tourist couples walked around reading each other's minds hardly speaking a word to each other.

Wide-eyed bedraggled conventioneers trying to find their hotels after staying out all night wandered lost and dazed.

Smiling newlyweds held hands, strolling down the streets, happy to be out of their hotel room after days of watching TV and ordering room service.

Joggers paced themselves down the street in their fashionable tank tops and shorts dodging dog poop in their state-of-the-art athletic shoes.

Aging retirees looking suspiciously like twins comparison shopped the restaurant lunch menus on their way to eat breakfast.

The scene replayed itself, day after day, year after year, like an old black and white movie.

Just before eight O'clock Johnny rang Dan Rice's doorbell. The wooden door was massive and looked to be very old with hand carved relief panels and wrought iron gargoyle accents.

Out of a shiny brass speaker box to the right of the door a woman's voice said, "Hello, may I help you?" Johnny gave his name and the door lock opened electronically. The speaker voice asked Johnny to please enter.

Johnny stepped into the foyer, pausing while his eyes adjusted to the dimly lit room. Elegant textures and exotic smells surrounded him. The furniture looked new, but the mahogany in the Louis XIV styling wore an ancient patina. Not a spec of dust rested anywhere.

Bronze sculptures of men and beast occupied the room, looking as if they would come to life when no one looked and stand still the moment anyone entered.

Johnny kept watch on them from the corner of his eyes just in case one might move. He was about to sit in a large overstuffed red Italian tapestry chair with dark wooden lions paw arms, when a well-dressed pert blond woman appeared in the dim light. She was wearing a fashionable dark gray business suit. Her perfect New Orleans accent caught Johnny's imagination the moment she spoke.

"Are you from Vieux Carre Architectural?" she asked.

"No Ma'am, my name is Johnny Thumper, I called yesterday morning," he said.

"Pardon me, sir. My name is Donna Sirgo, I'm Mr. Rice's assistant. Please follow me," she instructed.

"Thank you," Johnny said. He watched her disappear into the same dark hallway from which she had appeared. The hall was so dark, he hadn't realized it was there until she had interrupted his study of the foyer.

He followed her into a beautifully chandeliered waiting room then out through a set of ornate beveled cut-glass French doors that opened onto a private antique, hand-molded red brick courtyard. The courtyard was full of tropical plants and ferns and could have been featured in a gardening magazine.

A man, Johnny presumed, sat out in the courtyard by the fountain talking with a familiar-looking brunet woman dressed in a loose-fitting black outfit. He couldn't hear all of their conversation, but he did hear something about a Mercedes Benz dealership being converted into a restaurant, along with a lawsuit.

"Hello Mr. Thumper. It's a pleasure to meet you. I'm Dan Rice," he said. He walked toward Johnny, hand outstretched, wearing a black tailor-made suit and long sleeved white oxford cotton shirt with initialed gold cuff links.

"Hello Mr. Rice, I'm Johnny, Johnny Thumper. I would like to thank you for taking time to meet with me," he said. The woman excused herself, exiting with Donna.

"Mr. Thumper, I don't have a lot of time this morning. Could you tell me how you know Andrew?" he asked.

"Yes, sir, Andrew's wife Melanie and I are distant cousins," Johnny answered.

"If I may ask," Johnny said. "Mr. Rice, how are you and Andrew acquainted?" Dan Rice turned to look more fully at Johnny.

"Andrew didn't tell you?" Dan asked.

"No, sir," Johnny said. Dan Rice was a man in his late sixties, Johnny presumed, nowhere near Andrew's age.

"Andrew's father and I were close friends," Dan said. "You told my assistant Donna you had a tax matter to discuss with me?" Dan asked.

"Yes, sir, you see, uh, I really feel silly saying this," Johnny said. "But I've won the Florida State Lottery."

"Congratulations, Johnny," Dan said while sizing him up. Johnny wore his usual blue jeans and blue denim work shirt, shaggy hair and mustache.

"Thank you, Mr. Rice," Johnny said. "I haven't gotten the money yet. However, I have the ticket and I've confirmed the numbers with the lottery people. The reason I'm here is that I have an idea about taxes, and I thought you might be able to help me with it."

"Johnny, what is the sum we're talking about?" Dan said. He was apparently still trying to cut the meeting as short as possible. Johnny was unconformable with Dan's pretentious behavior, but he proceeded.

"Eighty-two million, sir," Johnny said. Johnny felt both embarrassed and proud at the same moment, using money to get someone's attention and/or approval was not his style. After all, this was a business meeting, he told himself. Dan Rice slowly stood straighter. Evidently, Johnny figured, he had sufficient funds to get Dan's attention.

"Would you like a cup of coffee?" Dan asked.

"No, thank you," Johnny said.

"Your tax responsibility on that sum of money would be quite substantial," Dan said. "The taxes on lotteries are typically taken out before they hand over the money. What specifically was your question?" He peered over his bi-focals at Johnny.

"Mr. Rice," Johnny said. "I need help setting up a non-profit corporation. I was wondering if a citizen of a foreign country were to win the lottery would he be liable for United States Federal or State income taxes?"

"I see what you're asking," Dan said. "If your hunch is correct what you're suggesting is that you'll become a resident of a tax haven and then claim your prize?"

"Yes," Johnny said. He could see that he'd finally gotten Dan Rice's full attention.

"What country, Mr. Thumper?" Dan asked.

"Belize or Costa Rica," Johnny said. "I believe they offer the tax haven benefits that I need."

"Yes, I'll check into it and get back to you," Mr. Rice said. "You plan on spending some of your winnings on charity?"

"Yes, sir, all that's humanly possible," Johnny said. Dan Rice shook Johnny's hand and showed Johnny to the courtyard door that led back out to Royal Street. If Dan Rice had not been a friend of Andrew's, Johnny thought, he would have found someone else to help him. Still he believed he could trust him as a lawyer so he would stick with him, at least now.

Since he was already in the French Quarter he figured he would look around a little while. He couldn't really help himself when it came to browsing in the Quarter. There are so many strange, one of a kind, unique places. Anyone with even a slight curiosity could waste a day nosing around. He headed for Jackson Square and the Louisiana State Museum, where he hadn't been in many years and was already anxious to get there again. Wandering came naturally to Johnny, too naturally he sometimes felt.

About lunchtime as Johnny was heading a couple of blocks out of the Quarter to Frenchman Street, for a cup of coffee, he recognized a musician he had seen recently walking toward him. Coco Robicheaux with a beautiful woman on his arm.

"Coco Robicheaux," Johnny said. Coco turned and looked at him smiling.

"Hey, how are you," Coco said with a smile.

"I saw you play at the House of Blues, the crowd loved you!" Johnny said. Coco smiled again at Johnny and replied "thanks we're going to a gig right now."

"Where?" Johnny asked.

"Margaritaville," Coco said. He shook Johnny's hand and walked on, Johnny turned and watched as the two of them seemed to float down Frenchman Street obviously in love. Johnny thought about how impressed he had been with Coco's song writing ability, about the lyrics, and about the almost hypnotic rhythmic spells that enchanted the audience that night. And he wished that one day he also could find his special God given talents so that he too could conjure and cast heaven inspired spells into the world rather than make poison nerve gas.

Johnny got home late that evening, much later than he had initially hoped at the start of the day. His beeper was beeping, evidently his beeper had finally dried out and started working okay again. He hadn't bothered to take it with him to the French Quarter believing it was ruined. Now it lay beeping on the galley table with six messages. This lottery business was really taking over Johnny's thoughts. He needed to get his head out of the clouds and his feet firmly on the ground. Getting his mind back to everyday living wouldn't be easy.

He decided he would return Lee's call first.

"Hello, JT," Lee's voice came over the telephone.

"Yeah, Lee, what's up?" Johnny said.

"What's up, what do you mean what's up?" Lee said. "Didn't you go down to the lottery office to collect your money?" Lee's voice jumped through the telephone line. Johnny cringed.

"No, no not yet," Johnny said. "I've got a few things I need to take care of first." He hated getting the third degree from anyone, but he had always allowed Lee leeway, being the old friends that they were.

"Man, you're going to screw around and mess this thing up somehow," Lee said. "Do you realize how much money 82 million dollars are? What you could do with that much money. Hell, you'd never have to work another day of your life."

"Yes, that's exactly what's holding me up," Johnny said. "I'm studying the tax burden right now. I could be moving south," Johnny said. He could almost hear Lee's mind working on the other end of the line.

"How would moving south help your tax burden?" Lee asked. "And what's more south than where you live now, I mean you live on a bay on the Gulf of Mexico?" His voice grew calmer while he tried to figure out what Johnny was up to.

"I'm still checking into it," Johnny said. "But if a non resident or non citizen wins the lottery without being in the state or country, then he may be able to avoid some or all of the income taxes, legally of course. I'm not sure yet."

"I refuse to believe you really won this thing, until you actually bank the money," Lee said. "Change the subject, we're still going down to Gulf Shores for the first week of November right?"

"Yeah, as far as I know," Johnny said. "Of all the lucky people in the world, I've got to be the luckiest. I keep expecting to wake up and find I've been dreaming up this lottery ticket thing."

"Yeah I don't believe it either," Lee said. "I still think your pulling the biggest practical of joke of your career."

"I peek at my winning lottery ticket every morning when I wake up," Johnny said.

"What do you mean peek at it?" Lee asked.

"I have to make sure it hasn't disappeared while I slept, that this all hasn't been some vision or dream" Johnny said. "Like the horse I dreamed my Aunt Betty gave me for my birthday when I was a kid."

"What are you talking about, JT?" Lee asked. Johnny's mind was naturally creative and Lee could never predict what would come out of it.

"In my dream as a kid," Johnny said. "I knew I was dreaming when my Aunt Betty gave me a horse. So for safekeeping I put my dream gift horse in the clothes closet, so it wouldn't wander off before I awakened." He wondered if Lee thought he was talking nonsense, because the telephone was silent.

"I still remember the feeling of disappointment when I opened that closet door the next morning," Johnny said. "I was really disappointed and felt rather foolish for it also."

"JT, you still sound foolish to me," Lee said.

"But, the lottery ticket is no dream," Johnny said. "Every morning when I wake up, I peek at it. I always find it safely sealed in its air tight sandwich bag."

"That's a good idea," Lee said. "Why not a safety deposit box?"

"I like the zip lock," Johnny said. "I can keep it close to me and just in case my boat sinks while I'm away, it'll stay dry." Johnny was proud of his innovative idea.

"Yeah, right, whatever. Keep me posted," Lee barked.

"All right, talk to you later," Johnny said.

Johnny called Virginia next to invite her to go sailing. They compared schedules and found out they could try to go sailing in the morning.

Johnny's alarm went off well before sunrise. He fixed a pot of fresh dark roast coffee, poured a tall cup, and went out to sit on the stern of the Dream Catcher to savor his morning and the invigorating black brew. He hoped the day would be a good day. The aroma from the coffee teased his taste buds as he waited for it to cool enough. There weren't many days perfect for sailing, conditions were a matter of chance. So far, the prospects were promising. The wind was blowing out of the northwest about ten to fifteen knots. Johnny could see every star in the sky, horizon to horizon. Not a cloud.

Too bad Virginia could not have come in last night, he thought. They could have gotten an earlier start and watched the sunrise from over the lake. He had seen the sun rise out on the water a few dozen times. Each time it left Johnny feeling he had witnessed a miracle.

He had taken his inflatable dinghy for a test ride last night to get some ice and cold drinks from the Rivermart and had noticed the air pressure was low. So in the darkness of the predawn morning he pressured it up.

His head still hurt when he bent over and his mind flashed back to the storm at the lighthouse. He rubbed the back of his head, it was still sore, and he could feel that a little blood had matted into his hair during the night.

"I'm as ready as can be," he thought. "If the wind would pick up a little more, everything will be wonderful."

Yesterday, before he called, Johnny didn't believe Virginia would come in for a sail. Her husband's condition also made Johnny hesitant about calling her, let alone becoming closer to her. But it appeared that she needed someone to be friends with and Johnny enjoyed talking to her. What the heck, he thought, you can't have too many friends.

The trouble was, he was so distracted with winning the lottery he didn't know if he would be good company on their sailing venture. Recently he'd made a commitment to himself to make time for making more friends in his life. He had only a few friends and he now owed it to himself to go on this sail.

He heard the floating dock squeak, and soft footsteps approaching in the promise of light, knowing it was Virginia before she appeared. Her fragrance drifted toward him on the north breeze. The fragrance, more than perfume, was hypnotic to him.

"Ahoy, Johnny," Virginia said. "Isn't it a beautiful day?" She wasn't sure what she was doing here. There wasn't any one thing that she could put her finger on. It had been years since Michael had gotten sick and anyone had asked her to go anywhere. Their friends that they had known as a couple had slowly drifted away from them, too disturbed by Michael's sickness to visit anymore. Virginia herself had never come to terms with her and Naichie's need for companionship, preferring to stay home and mourn. Eventually Virginia's mother and sisters interceded, concerned about her health, and forced her to start getting out some, to live again.

She honestly had never thought she would see Johnny again until yesterday, just a few days after they had met and he called to ask her to go sailing. She had enjoyed talking with him the other night. She had even believed their meeting had more to do with being kindred souls than just a chance conversation. She didn't want Johnny to think she was actually going on dates because she wasn't and after all she was a married woman. But something in her heart told her that there was something special about Johnny and she had encouraged him.

"Hi, Virginia," Johnny said. "What do you mean a beautiful day, it's still dark?" Virginia was wearing a loose fitting long-sleeved white cotton shirt to keep the sun off, a pair of baggy faded blue jeans with holes in the knees, and a pair of deck shoes, well broken in. Her long silky black hair was pulled back into a French braided pony tail. It glistened in the remaining moonlight.

"If we hurry, we can watch the sunrise over the lake this morning." Johnny said. "Please come aboard." He leaned over the port side of the boat to help her aboard sticking his large tanned hand out to hold her bag. "Here Virginia, hand me your bag," Johnny said. "How was your trip?" She lifted her bag toward his waiting hand. Grabbing it, he swivelled his torso around setting her bag on the deck next to the stern wheel. The night they had met he had wanted to reach out to hug her goodbye but hadn't. The feeling was there now. He was attracted to her, and this made him uncomfortable. He had to keep reminding himself that she was married. Virginia reached for him and gave him a firm hug.

"Welcome aboard," Johnny mumbled, her perfume thick in his nostrils.

"Thank you Captain," Virginia said. "Not a bad trip, I woke up about three and was on the road by three thirty. What time is it now?" She set her right foot on the port side toe rail and he pulled her up. She stepped down on the aft deck and looked around smiling nervously, looking a little bit unsure of what to do next.

"That fresh coffee smells great," she said. "Got any for the crew?"

"Sure," he said. "You take cream and sugar?" Virginia nodded her head yes, Johnny smiled and disappeared down to the galley and returned less than a minute later with her order.

"It's almost six o'clock," he said. "How long can you stay?" That was an awkward question he thought after he had said it. "What time do you need to be back home? So I'll have some idea what our agenda might be." She gave him a relaxed smile, while she thought about the question and sipped her coffee.

"If we come in late, I'll stay at a friend's in New Orleans," Virginia said. "Let's just see how things go-you know I've never been sailing before."

"No, I didn't know that," Johnny said. "We don't have to take the boat out sailing if you're uncomfortable. We could just motor up the river."

"No, if you think the weather is safe," Virginia said, "Then I'll be disappointed if we don't go out." She was trying to smile as she looked for her sea legs. Johnny picked up her bag, his empty coffee cup, and opened the cabin hatch leading into the galley.

"OK, let me show you around before we get under way," he said. He stepped down into the boat's pilot house cabin and showed her where the "head" was and how the toilet worked, how to call for help on the VHF radio in case something would happen to him and where the fire extinguishers were located.

He set out the blue seat cushions on the bench seats and took out two life jackets. Virginia put hers on and he tried not to smile as she tried to figure out the straps. He cast off the dock lines and backed the boat out of the slip using the 50 horse power diesel engine. Johnny worked the boat as if Virginia wasn't on board. He didn't want to give her any responsibilities, not until she felt comfortable enough to ask to help.

"This is a satellite signaling device," he said. He pointed to a cylindrical shaped, orange piece of plastic equipment hanging on the handrail. "If we should get into serious trouble and need help, if we couldn't raise anyone on the radios, then we would turn this on here, like this." Her eyes opened wide and followed his pointed fingers as she pondered the possibilities of what he had just said.

"What would happen then?" she asked. He smiled and realized he might be scaring her.

"It's a transmitter. It alerts the authorities by satellite that we are in distress," he said. "It's a wonderful safety device that's hardly ever used."

It wasn't long before the Dream Catcher rounded the last channel marker of the river. The sun had just cleared the horizon as the boat created the only ripples in the muddy-colored lake water. The brackish lake was as smooth as glass. Johnny doubted if the slight breeze would be enough to push the boat but he unfastened the roller furling and released the jib anyway.

"OK, if you'll sit over here, I'll set the jib," he said. She moved to the starboard side and watched as he unrolled the tall white satin looking sail bordered with coarse blue sacrificial cloth.

Virginia didn't normally get this far from home on a weekday, but her conversation with JT last week made her curious as to who Johnny Thumper was. He didn't appear to be married or marriage minded, but she wasn't looking for a husband anyway. What she needed more than anything was adult companionship. Since her husband had been sick, most of her time had been spent taking care of Naichie and him. Now that Michael was being taken care of in a nursing home, she stayed close to home. She still hoped that someday a miracle might happen and she would get a telephone call saying her husband had asked for her.

Johnny was unlike most men she'd met. He reminded her of Michael, a strong-willed person, but one she could trust. She tilted her head back looking at the limp sail then checked the sky for a storm. There wasn't a cloud. The boat gently leaned forward and stopped.

"Damn, I think the boat's stuck," Johnny said. "I forgot to turn on the depth finder's alarm." He looked at the sonar and turned it on. It beeped a shallow water warning.

"Yeah we're stuck."

It had been sudden, almost as if she were dreaming, the way Johnny appeared in front of her on the stairs that night. She'd been in deep thought about visiting her sick husband in the nursing home that day. The treatments for his brain cancer had done more damage to him than the doctors had predicted. He was unable to talk or take care for himself now. She found it hard lately, going to see him. Visiting him now was extremely depressing.

Naichie, her son, had been struggling with his father's illness as well. As time slipped by they realized with dreaded certainty that he would never be well again.

The weak breeze attempted to fill the boat's sails. It fluttered, making a sound like the flopping of fresh sheets to make a bed. It was obvious there wasn't going to be enough wind to sail that day, at least not this morning. He rolled up the sail and put the engine in reverse.

"Is there anything I can do to help?" Virginia asked.

"Virginia, I hate to tell you but, sailing is not going to be an option this morning," he said. "It doesn't have to be a complete loss though." He was trying to think of a constructive way to enjoy their time together. After all, she had driven hours to go sailing. Johnny raced the engine up to maximum rpm's, but the Dream Catcher sat there like a helpless, beached, whale.

Johnny thought Virginia might be having a panic attack. She was very quiet and her knuckles were turning white as she squeezed the ties on her life jacket. Johnny went through his options quietly in his mind. He could call a tow on the radio to pull him off or row out in his dinghy, set his anchor and winch them back off the mud flat. First, he would have to settle her nerves so she could help him.

"I've brought some fresh tuna steaks to grill for lunch," he said. She looked at him with a blank face. "We can anchor at the sand bar over there." He pointed to the mouth of the river, to a wide uninhabited sandy beach accessible only by use of a boat. "In the summer time there would have been as many as fifty people sunning there. Do you fish?"

"I haven't fished since I was a little girl," she said, "When my sisters and I would go visit our father on Dolphin Island. He's got a beautiful house there on the water. But he never really had much time for us, his children from his first marriage." She was still feeling disappointment after all these years.

"Well, I'm not very good at fishing either," Johnny said. "But we can give it a try, if you'd like?"

"Sure," She said, forcing a smile. A passing tug boat sent a foot-tall wake onto the Dream Catcher's starboard side gently pushing and lifting her off the mud flat back into the deeper channel. Virginia clapped as Johnny spun the Dream Catcher around and headed for the sandbar. He set the anchor near the shore and watched until he was sure the boat would stay.

The sun rose slowly over Lake Pontchartrain warming the cool morning air, Johnny took off his shirt to catch some early morning rays. Virginia casually glanced at him as he pulled his cotton shirt over his head and saw that his torso was tanned, tightly fitted and toned. Johnny was in good shape.

"Would you like me to put sun screen on you?" Virginia asked. Johnny turned to her with a surprised blush on his face. It had been a long time since a woman had touched him.

"Oh, ah, thanks but I've already got a pretty good tan, I don't believe I'll need any," Johnny said. Virginia giggled.

"Oh, come on, I promise I won't hurt you," Virginia said. Johnny, still blushing offered his back to her, hoping that she had not realized that he was embarrassed. Virginia opened the tube of sun screen and squirted the lotion into her left hand and rubbed her hands together. She slowly spread the white cream, caressing Johnny's tanned back as she worked down to the point where the elastic on his swimsuit clung to his waistline. Johnny stood motionless as she worked the lotion onto his back, then triceps and forearms. He could feel her touch lingering around his arms squeezing the lotion into each muscle as if she were giving him a massage. Finally, as Johnny thought she was finished, he felt her flip the elastic waistband of his shorts.

"Just what I was afraid of," Virginia said.

"What!" Johnny squealed, suddenly even more embarrassed at the pitch of his voice. "What are you doing?" he looked over his shoulder at her sitting there on the cushion grinning at him as she squeezed more lotion on her hands. Johnny could feel his heart pounding. He was so attracted to Virginia that her touch was more than distracting.

"This cute little waist of yours is going to get all pink and red if you don't stand still," Virginia said. She was almost as excited by this game of tease as he was. She thought it was cute that Johnny seemed ticklish and was enjoying feeling him squirm while she gently finished rubbing the sun screen around his shorts.

Johnny dove into the water and bobbed his head up quickly to look at Virginia.

"I hope this stuff is water proof," he said. Virginia gave him a pouty-faced look.

"What about me," Virginia teased. "I was hoping you would return the favor and rub some on me."

"Toss it to me," Johnny replied. "I'll put some on you at the sand bar." Johnny was stalling hoping to could calm himself down before they climbed onto the sand.

Virginia stood up and unbuckled her life jacket, peeled off her shirt and jeans revealing her swim suit. She peeked at Johnny through her silky hair as it fanned across her cheek hiding her mischievous eyes while she neatly folded her clothes. His gaze was locked onto her every movement as she finished and dove into the water.

They swam to the sand bar and built a sand castle. The wind remained calm and the fish weren't biting. After swimming and talking the morning away, they swam back to the boat for lunch. Their conversation was enjoyable for both of them and time passed by much too quickly considering their mutual desire to know each other better.

He brought the boat back into the marina early that afternoon so Virginia could make it home before dark. As they said goodbye Virginia gave him a long hug.

"I still owe you a sail," Johnny promised.

"Yeah, thank God that boat came by with that big wake or we'd still be sitting in the channel," she said.

He smiled at her comment, handed her bag over the handrail, and watched as she walked away down the dock.

TELL ME WHAT YOU WANT AND I'LL SHOW YOU WHO YOU ARE

"Mister President, how the hell do you think we raise money around here anyway?" Senator Redhead asked. He was steaming mad at the freshman President. "Do you think the public would have ever heard of you if our very generous friends hadn't backed your campaign?" The telephone remained silent as both men considered their next move.

"Look, Dick, you know me," the President said. "Hell, I'm as concerned about party lines as the next guy. But environmental concerns are big in the public opinion polls right now. Global warming may be real or it may not, I don't know. University-backed scientific advisors tell me this last century has been the hottest the planet has experienced in the last six thousand years. Industry-backed studies show the opposite, and, frankly, I don't care one way or the other. What is important though is getting the American people to believe we care."

"OK, all right," Senator Redhead said. "Just don't forget which side your bread is buttered on." Dick Redhead could tolerate a lot of things from the new President, but pissing off big campaign contributors could be deadly to everyone in the party. Dick hung up the telephone and looked at his watch: eight o'clock in the morning Washington, D.C. That made it five o'clock at his ranch in the northern California mountains.

His father had made a living there as did his grandfather and his great-grandfather all the way back to the Gold Rush days of the 1850's. Dick Redhead's ancestors had fought for the land. They had fought off claim jumpers, outlaws, squatters, and Indians. The Indians had been the most persistent, wiping out two of his great uncles before the turn of the century. After those killings, Dick's great-grandfather put a bounty on the surviving Indians living on the Redhead lumber company's holdings. By the early 1900's the last of the native threats to their family land had been wiped out.

Dick's family had fought for their sixteen square miles of wooded mountainsides for over one hundred and fifty years, earning their living through minerals, and lumber. Their logging company had made them multimillionaires and, for generations, nothing had gotten in their way. Now overcoming all those odds, a damn bird was shutting down California's timber industry.

Senator Redhead had been in Washington a lot longer than the President of the United States had, and he figured he would be there long after the President had gone back South.

He'd take care of those environmentalists, like his grandfather had taken care of those Indians, if he had too. But nobody was going to wipe out the Redhead holdings, not while Dick Redhead was alive anyway.

Naichie could hear the telephone ringing in his mother's bedroom. He opened his eyes and spotted the dim morning light filtering through his blue bedroom curtains. It was too early for his mother's employer to be calling. He wondered as he listened to his mother's hushed telephone conversation in the other room. Her voice was sad.

A sympathetic tear formed in the corner of his eye and he pulled his blankets back over his head hoping to go back to sleep.

Silently he slipped out of his low single youth bed. His father had taken the sleep rails off it before he had gone into the hospital. Naichie still had his father's screw driver hidden under his mattress hoping that one day he could show his father that he'd saved the screw driver for him and he hadn't lost it. He slipped his blue cartoon character bedroom slippers on and silently walked to his mother's bedroom door. Reaching up, he slowly turned the doorknob. It felt of cool metal on his tiny fingers. His mother was sat on the side of her bed, her bedside lamp was on the light form framing her in silhouette, She smiled sleepily at him as he came toward her bed, dragging his favorite blanket along beside him.

"Mamma," Naichie said. "Are you all right?"

Virginia finished her conversation and hung up the telephone. She picked up her little boy, hugged him to her breast and pulled him into her lap straightening his shiny tossed hair. He was still her tiny baby although he seemed a little bigger every morning.

"Mamma, who was that on the telephone?" he said.

"That was the nurse who takes care of Daddy," she said. "She said that he had a bad night last night, but he's better right now."

"Can we go see Daddy today?" he asked. His mother shifted him to her bed and covered him up to his tiny chin with her still warm thick quilt.

"Of course," she said. "After you get out of school today, I'll pick you up from the sitter's early so we can go visit Daddy." He smiled as his mother gave him a gentle kiss on his sleep-swollen cheek.

"Now you can still get another hour of sleep if you want to," she said. "When you wake up again I'll have some biscuits and jelly for you." He smiled again, rolled over, and fell back to sleep before Virginia even walked out of the door.

Johnny had forgotten to call Karen back the other night. He knew she wouldn't be too upset with him. After all, it wasn't unusual for him to do that. She had been trying to fix him up with a wife for years. They had grown up next door to each other and she was the closest thing he would ever have to a real sister.

He wanted to tell her about the lottery, but he knew it was beyond her ability to keep it a secret. The thought of that much money would make her lose sleep at night. Somehow he would have to at least give her a hint or when she really did find out about it she would mistake his silence for greed.

"Hello, Karen, how are you doing?" he began.

"Fine, Johnny, and how are you," she said.

"Great, Karen, everything is going great," he said. "How are my nephew and niece?" he asked. They weren't really his niece and nephew by blood but he had claimed them as such from birth.

"They're fine, Johnny. Is something wrong?" she said. She could sense a difference in his voice.

"No, no, everything is fine, better than ever," he said. "Uh, look, I may be going on a trip soon so I wanted to make sure everyone is all right and to see if y'all need anything?"

"No, Johnny, everything is going fine," she said. "Doing better this year with the Bed and Breakfast better than any year before. It's been picking up steadily ever since you helped us open it." She was wondering what he was up to.

"That's great, Karen," he said. "I'm not trying to get personal or anything but I'm probably going to have some extra money coming in this year and I just wanted to know if there is anything you might need. You know, that would make your life a little easier for you." Her suspicions deepened, but she decided to play along to see what was the joke.

"Johnny, the college tuition for the kids puts a little strain on our budget as always, and I'd love to take Mom and Dad on a vacation you know if I had some extra money," she said. Then she laughed at Johnny's preposterous offer. "But there's always something, and you know you don't owe us anything." Annie, the housekeeper, passed by her with the linen for the guest cottage. Karen moved to the side of the kitchen counter island to let her by.

"Yeah, I know I don't owe you anything," he said. "But if things work out for me, I'll send you and your Mom, and Dad wherever y'all want to go on vacation, within reason." He still wasn't laying his cards on the table, but she didn't want to look the gift horse in the mouth.

"Johnny, what's going on?" she said.

"Nothing really," he said. "I just want to make sure you're doing well. I've got to go for now but be thinking about where you would like to go on vacation next fall."

"Well, that depends on the budget!" she said. She was enjoying the game of cat and mouse. They had known each other since before memory and he had always been a practical joker. Saying the word vacation in front of Karen was like waving a red flag in front of a bull.

"If you could take your Mom anywhere in the world, where would that be?" he asked.

"Hawaii, without a doubt," she quickly said before he could refill his lungs with air.

"Then I suggest you call Leslie in Baton Rouge, at the House of Travel in the next few months," he said. "And get her to start researching. Stay anywhere you like you know within reason."

"Johnny, you know you're crazy," she laughed. She didn't know what Johnny was up to but at this point she didn't care or quite believe him either. He had been known to play practical jokes before but this was beyond the scope of any he'd done before.

"Yeah, all the girls tell me that," he said.

"Bye," she said. She was worried about him. He should have been married years ago and he could still easily find a suitable wife, a young professional girl in her early thirties, one who could give him the children he needed. Karen picked up the telephone and called her mother.

Since Johnny had to go back to the chemical plant the next day he decided to use the rest of his day to make phone calls and take care of his boat. He was sure Karen was on the telephone right now with her mother. The two of them would be discussing ways to get him married so he could raise some children. It seemed to Johnny that's about all she thought about when she thought of him. Children, children, and children. He wouldn't mind children, truly he loved them, but he certainly wasn't going to get married just to raise children. He was too much of a romantic for that.

He walked into the Crosswinds, got himself a glass of wine, and came back outside to the pay telephone. He put the coins in and sat in the weathered restaurant chair. He wanted to get his boat ready for the possible trip south.

"Hello, Madisonville Boat Yard? May I speak with Clay Fields?" he said.

"Is that you, Johnny?" he heard Clint, the yard foreman, say.

"Yeah, Damn I haven't talked to you since the summer, Clint, how in the hell did you know, it was me?"

"Just a minute, Johnny, I'll get Clay," he said. Johnny heard him lay the telephone down. A couple of minutes later he heard Clay pick up the telephone.

"Hello Johnny," Clay said. "I thought you were going to come in months ago so we could do a bottom job on the Dream Catcher."

"Yeah, well you know, Mr. Fields there's never enough time or money to do everything," he said. "But now I need more than a bottom job. I want you to repair some bottom blisters, paint the topsides and a few other things. I'm fixing to take her out for a spin."

"Oh, really, where to?" Mr. Fields said. Johnny almost said Belize but decided against it.

"I'm not saying, just yet," he said. "But I'll be gone for a while. Mr. Clay, would you mind calling West Wind Sails and ask them to meet me at the yard next Saturday? I need to get a couple of sails made and some repairs, too."

"You'd better call them yourself, Mr. Thumper," Clay said. "About what time will you come in?"

"Early, Clay," he said. "I'm not sleeping very late these days."

"Okay Johnny, I'll be watching for you," Clay said and hung up the telephone.

Johnny was an excellent swimmer, and as long as he could see land he felt safe. However, sailing to the Yucatan would put him outside the view of land and the reach of the Coast Guard, so he wanted to be sure the Dream Catcher was shipshape.

Once the Dream Catcher was ready, once he could get his hands on the lottery money, he would have to resign from his job. That would be hard, he had been working there for fifteen years. Just thinking about not having a job sent butterflies to his stomach. But he would know when the time was right, he told himself, he just had to wait for all the pieces to come together.

THERE ARE NO COINCIDENCE

Johnny didn't have anything planned for Christmas. He figured everyone would meet at Karen's house. Her family and friends would meet for the annual Christmas party. He could show up at the party and get all of his visiting over with, everyone in one spot, all in one night.

Johnny turned off the shower and reached for his towel, still damp from use the night before. He carefully dried his body and wiped off the tiny medicine cabinet mirror. Sliding back the mahogany paneled door on the cabinet, he slipped the hairbrush through his wet tangled hair. Making sure that it was straight just the way his father taught him to do as a child.

He stepped out of the tiny room and closed the door behind him to keep the humid air out of the rest of the boat. He threw the wet towel down on the teak and holly floor, mopping up the water that always found its way out of the shower. He opened the clothes closet door. There was one dark gray suit for weddings and funerals, one pressed white shirt, a silk tie his niece Becky had given him for Christmas, one pair of khaki pants, one brown work belt, one black dress belt, two pairs of blue jeans and two denim work shirts.

He reached into the tiny packed closet, pulled out the pressed white dress shirt and khaki pant and slipped them on. Putting on his dress pair of boat shoes he walked out to the marina pay phone and called Karen's Carnot Posey Bed and Breakfast.

Confederate General Carnot Posey had built the place. He lived there from 1845 until he was wounded in a Virginia battle during the Civil War in 1863 and then died a few days later.

Posey and Jefferson Davis, the President of the Confederacy, had been friends. They'd fought and were wounded in the Mexican war together. Karen's research showed that Carnot had been an U.S. Attorney, and a planter. Johnny had heard Karen give the tour dozens of times over the years when he visited.

There were only a few stores in Woodville, so Johnny usually shopped for Karen on his way up to the Posey House. Today, she had asked him to stop at Maison Blanche to pick up a dress for a guest at the Bed and Breakfast. That was the strangest shopping request he'd ever gotten from her, but he gladly obliged.

He parked near the mall entrance of the department store and began looking for the dress department. He asked guidance from several young women working at the cosmetics counter. Looking at them he couldn't tell how much was real or how much was makeup, but the girls looked very pretty. Johnny figured he'd have to scrub them up pretty good to find out what they really looked like.

It wasn't long before he realized he didn't know whose dress he was supposed to pick up. The sales clerk insisted she didn't have a dress for Karen so Johnny called Karen to ask.

"Karen, I'm at Maison Blanche's now and they insist they don't have a dress under your name?" he said. Karen apologized, saying that she had forgotten to tell Johnny the name.

"The dress is under the name Virginia Forest," she said.

"Virginia Forest?" he said. "I know her. She's from Alabama, right?"

"Yes, that's right," Karen said. "She checked in Monday for three days, but at breakfast Tuesday we got to talking and she said she knew you. She said you were the one who told her about the Carnot Posey House. That's why she came for a visit," she said.

"Yeah, that's right," Johnny said.

"Virginia didn't realize you were coming in for Christmas," Karen said. "So I asked her to stay through Saturday as my guest. That way y'all can visit, I hope you don't mind? She seems very nice."

"No, I don't mind," he said. "Virginia's a very nice person. It will be good to see her."

"That's good." Karen said. "Because I wasn't going to ask her to leave."

"O.K. I'm getting the dress and heading straight up from here. See you in a little while," he said.

The drive out from Madisonville was normally two hours to Woodville, Mississippi, but today it took him twice as long. When he finally arrived at the antebellum home, across from the oldest newspaper in Mississippi, guest cars were parked up and down the entire length of Church Street and Second South. Karen had told Johnny to invite his friends from work, but he'd forgotten to mention it until the last minute. He didn't know who all had been invited, but he did notice Lee's car down the street.

Johnny was sharing a room with Karen's son Curt up in the attic. That's how a person could tell their standing in importance on Karen's guest list. The lesser the accommodations the greater the number of more important people were spending the night.

Usually only Karen's family stayed the night of the Christmas Party unless a friend was coming in from a great distance, then Karen would make room. Johnny was surprised that Karen had invited Virginia to stay for whatever reason.

He found a parking spot just down the street in front of the old 1870's Catholic Church and parked his car. He grabbed the presents from the trunk, stacked them on top of Virginia's dress box, headed down Church Street to Second South, and took a left. Stepping over the curb, he stepped onto the golden Ginkgo Biloba leaves that covered the lawn like a yellow carpet of snow and headed toward the front door.

Curt came running out to meet Johnny. He was 21 years old, six feet, two inches tall, and a recent graduate from LSU, still glad to see Johnny. It gave Johnny a great feeling.

"Uncle Johnny, you're getting shorter every time I see you," Curt said.

"Thanks a lot, you want to help me with these boxes, Mr. Big Guy," Johnny teased. Curt nodded his head, and Johnny handed him all but the dress box.

"Did you get to meet Virginia?" he asked Curt.

"Yes sir, Uncle Johnny, she sure is a nice woman," Curt said. He had a big grin. "You and her going steady or anything?"

"No, no, she's just a friend of mine, I didn't even know she was going to be here," Johnny said. "Do you know where she is? I need to give this box to her."

Curt pointed to the guesthouse behind the big house, and said he believed she was there. Johnny told Curt he'd see him later and walked over to the guesthouse carrying the dress box.

Furlee, the gray and white tabby, jumped off the steps when she saw Johnny coming and ran to his side to escort him along the way. Furlee was a mean, grumpy, hard-headed old female cat who had never had a litter of kittens. She could stand off a hundred-pound German Shepherd. If you would help her start a dog moving away, she would chase it to the edge of the yard.

Knocking on the guesthouse door he heard Virginia's voice answer hello through the old cypress door.

"It's Johnny, Johnny Thumper," he said. He heard Virginia's muffled footsteps on the old oak floorboards of the converted gardeners quarters . She gave him a giant grin and reached out for a hug.

"I know this looks like I'm tracking you down but that's not it at all," she said.

"It never passed through my mind," he smiled back at her. "Karen told me you were expecting to leave Wednesday but that she talked you into staying until tomorrow."

"That's what happened," she said, "Girl Scout's honor. I had no idea that you were coming to visit this weekend. I was, I mean, I really needed to get away from my everyday routine. So, I thought I would visit your friend's Bed and Breakfast. Remember you told me about it last October?"

"Was it that long ago that we went sailing?" he asked. She continued to smile, knowing that in his own way he was apologizing. "I've been really busy getting Dream Catcher ready for an extended sailing trip."

"If you'll remember, we didn't go sailing," she said. She smiled bigger and asked him to come in. Following her directions he set her dress box on the couch. She sat in the chair facing the couch and asked him to be seated.

"Would you like a soft drink or I've got a bottle of red wine Karen gave me this afternoon?" she said. "How about having a glass with me?" Johnny nodded his head.

"I haven't said hello to anyone yet but Curt," he smiled. "But surely it wouldn't hurt to relax a little after traveling half a day to get here."

"I hope it wasn't too much trouble for you to pick up my dress?" she asked. He looked at her and smiled trying to hide his thoughts from her.

"Not at all," he replied. "But I do believe it's the first time in my life I've bought a dress." They both laughed hard as she poured the Merlot into two crystal wineglasses, Johnny said thanks, relieved to have arrived, and held up his wineglass.

"A toast! May the cheer and goodwill of Christmas last all year long!" Johnny said. Their glasses tipped with a ring of harmony and they each sipped the room-temperature blend of a grape harvest from years ago in a vineyard half way around the world.

"You haven't been to Orange Beach lately?" she asked. He shifted in his seat a little not wanting to break eye contact. He'd wanted to call her several times but had procrastinated and time eventually had slipped away from him.

"No, I haven't," he said. "I don't usually get down there but two or three times a year. I always try to make the Song Writers Festival and usually once or twice more than that," he said. Her eyes dropped to the floor. Although they had only known each other a short time she found herself jealous of his time away from her.

"How's your husband doing?" he asked. "Any improvements?"

"No, if anything his condition has worsened," she said. "Are you still reading about American Indian culture?" she asked.

"Yeah, I would like to spend some time with a native teacher or in a community of American Indians one of these days," he said. "One of my great-grandmothers was an American Indian. Their religious practices seem so different from the traditional worship that Christians practice. I guess it all depends on how you were raised as to what seems normal."

"Yes, everyone sticks pretty much to their comfort zone, how they were raised," she said.

"Do you know of any communities where a person could live within the culture?" he asked. Virginia said she didn't, but an American Indian Medicine Man she knew up in Taos, New Mexico, might be willing to guide Johnny through some of their religious ceremonies. His name was White Deer, and Virginia believed he still lived in or near the Taos Pueblo.

"Virginia, do you like to ride motorcycles?" he asked. Virginia's face lit up but Johnny didn't see it. He was deep in thought.

"I used to ride with my husband," she sighed and Johnny turned his attention back to Virginia. "He used to have a Harley Davidson before we were married but I sold it after he went into the nursing home. We needed the money. Do you have a bike?" she said.

"Sure do, motorcycle ownership runs in my family,"Johnny's face lit up with a big smile. "My father had a couple of Harley Davidson motorcycles and an Indian back in the forties and fifties. I bought an FXR back in 1993 and I still have it. I even have my father's leather World War One flyer's cap and jacket, I wear them sometimes when I ride."

"Really," Virginia laughed at him.

"A couple of guys from work want me to go up to Taos in May," he said. "You could come along or meet us up there. Then we could visit White Deer." Virginia appeared to be considering the proposition when a knock broke her train of thought. She got up to answer the door.

"Have you seen Johnny?" Karen said. Johnny recognized Karen's voice from out on the red brick porch of the guesthouse.

"I'm not holding him against his will, I promise," Virginia laughed. "Please come in." Johnny stood up and hugged Karen.

Virginia poured a glass of wine for Karen. Karen told Johnny that if he wanted to take a shower before cocktails began, now was a good time. He remembered to finally tell Virginia that the box on the couch had her dress in it and she thanked him again for stopping at Maison Blanche. Johnny told her if she wanted to return it, she was on her own. Virginia and Karen laughed and both said thanks again. Johnny set his empty wine glass next to the now-empty bottle and excused himself. After Johnny left, the two women began to talk about what they were going to wear that evening. Karen offered Virginia whatever accessories she might need.

It was getting dark outside now as Johnny headed across the driveway to the main house.

"Uncle Johnny," Curt called. Johnny heard his hushed voice come from the kitchen as he walked into the back of the old home. Curt was sitting at the kitchen counter island.

"Oh, hey, Curt, what are you sneaking around for?" he said.

"I'm not sneaking around, I just didn't want anyone else to hear me," Curt said.

"Sounds like sneaking to me," he laughed. "What did you want to tell me?"

"There's a hidden room upstairs," Curt said. "Did you know?"

"No, I didn't," he said. "Where upstairs?"

"It's up in the attic," Curt said. "If you've got time now, I'll show you." Curt stood up and started walking toward the sun-porch and the steep stairs leading up to the attic.

Curt walked past his sister, Becky. Johnny didn't recognize her. At nineteen she looked like Miss America in her evening gown.

"Hi, Uncle Johnny," Becky said. Johnny stared for several long seconds his face turned a shade of red, as he finally recognized her.

"Becky, I've never seen you wear make-up before," he said. "You're all grown up!"

"Oh, Uncle Johnny, you're always full of compliments, aren't you?" Becky blushed. "Let me introduce you to my boyfriend." Johnny's jaw dropped at the thought of little Becky having a boyfriend.

"Uncle Johnny, this is Robby," Becky said. "Robby, this is my Uncle Johnny." Johnny shook the young boy's hand and told him to behave himself.

"Uncle Johnny," Becky said. "Robby's in medical school. He's going to be a Pediatrician." When Johnny asked the boy how old he was and the boy replied twenty-two, Johnny was once again reminded how fast life was whirling past him.

Curt elbowed Johnny, Johnny told Robby it was a pleasure to meet him and that he would talk with them later. Curt led Johnny up into the upstairs living quarters, past Johnny's backpack leaning against the wall and they turned heading toward the southern section attic overlooking the back yard and horse pasture.

"I don't know why anyone in our family's never found the room before," Curt said. "I just found it this week while looking for my old BB gun."

"Other than the attic being big enough to build a house in," Johnny said. "I guess no one ever wandered over here since your mom and dad bought the place."

Curt led Johnny toward a louvered gable that overlooked the back yard. Directly to the right of it was a ten-by six-foot room that opened into the floor of the attic. Curt climbed down into the room and Johnny followed.

"Uncle Johnny, what do you think they used this for?" Curt said.

"This house dates back to the Indian Wars," he said. "This town is really near the beginning of the old Natchez Trace which had hostile Indians and highway robbers, my guess would be this room was for hiding if they were in danger," he speculated.

Curt reached into a corner of the tiny room and picked up a small dusty wooden box which they opened and found several small old leather bags tied together at the top with a worn leather strap. When the strap was untied they found cedar chips in one and some light herbal-smelling plant leaves in the others.

"What is it, Uncle Johnny?" Curt said. Johnny shrugged his shoulders.

"I don't have any idea," he said.

"They're prayer ties," Virginia said. Her voice came from over their heads. Curt and Johnny bumped into each other trying to see who was talking to them.

"Sorry," she said, "I didn't mean to scare you guys. Becky overheard your plans and showed me where to find you." Johnny and Curt stood frozen. "I see you still haven't showered or changed clothes yet?" Virginia said to Johnny.

"No, I haven't. If you ever scare me like that again, I promise I'll scream," he said. Virginia laughed. She really felt strongly that God had put them together, both on that night in Florida and tonight, here. She wished she could know what to do with the strong emotions she felt every time she saw Johnny.

"Prayer ties, what or should I ask, who uses them?" he asked.

"American Indians," she said. "Someone evidently used this room for a hiding place to keep sacred things."

"Hey, Uncle Johnny," Curt said. "Out in the old water well house we found a hand-carved bow but no arrows. I was going to put a string on the bow and shoot it, but my dad nearly pitched a fit. I put it away in the guest house closet where Miss Virginia's staying."

"I'd better take a shower," Johnny said. Johnny climbed out of the little hiding place, and excused himself, tracing his footsteps back, he found his back pack and carried it to the shower in Curt's room. As he unpacked he realized how stupid he was to have put his extra clothes in it. They were all wrinkled now. Luckily, the clothes he had on were still clean so he took a shower and put them back on.

The Christmas party went on until the early morning hours with the local guest leaving first, at around ten, then the friends from Baton Rouge leaving before twelve, and finally, only family and friends who were spending the night at the Carnot Posey House remained. Virginia's red dress had been the prettiest dress at the Christmas party. She told Karen that she would have never bought it for herself had she seen it before she owned it.

Lee had brought along a beautiful date named Dana and had hardly taken time to talk to Johnny the entire evening. Johnny was surprised that Lee hadn't try to ask him about the lottery ticket, but it appeared Dana had him well distracted.

Johnny walked Virginia back outside to the guesthouse. She yawned as Johnny opened the guest cottage door for her.

"I don't think I should really consider traveling with you guys to Taos, but I'm flattered that you asked," she said.

"I didn't think you really would but the offer is real if you should change your mind," he offered.

"When you know for sure if you're going call me and I'll write White Deer a letter," she said. "I'll let him know that you would like to see him."

"Thanks," he said, "and good night."

Virginia leaned forward reaching out for Johnny. She pulled him close to her and pressed him with a gentle, long hug. Johnny froze, not knowing what to do, he just held her gently for long seconds, smelling her perfumed hair and feeling her womanly body leaning close him. They were on dangerous territory. He wanted her and obviously she wanted him. But how, and what were the rules for such a situation? He wondered if he should say "if only you weren't married," that didn't seem fair. Hadn't she promised in front of God "in sickness and in health?" Was a spouse in a vegetable state, artificially kept alive, really alive? Wouldn't it only complicate things to say "I love you, but we'll have to wait until your husband dies?"

Johnny awoke as the sun was rising, lying on top of the goose down comforter. Virginia and he were still locked in tight embrace, she with her back pressed into his front. He knew this before he opened his eyes. He could feel the gentle rise and fall of her breathing and smell her fragrance, their arms and legs intimately locked into complete surrender of their separate identities. Johnny opened his eyes and found them in the middle of the guest cottage's king-size bed still wearing their now wrinkled party clothes. As gently as possible Johnny trying not to wake Virginia, he moved away from her. She opened her eyes slightly.

"Please don't leave me," Virginia pleaded. Johnny felt his heart swell with emotion. Virginia could sense he was about to cry.

"I don't want anyone to think the wrong thing," Johnny said.

"I don't care," Virginia said. Johnny's voice was shaking.

"Yes you do Virginia, Karen will serve brunch about ten-thirty. I'll see you then." Virginia closed her eyes.

Johnny walked back toward the big house. All the lights were still off as he stumbled his way through the still darkness searching for safe footing. Furlee bumped against his leg, startling him.

"Damn you, Furlee, you scared the hell out of me," he said. Furlee meowed as Johnny bent over and picked her up. "I guess you want in the house, right?" He carried her into the kitchen and set her down on the floor. "Now look, you, if you get in trouble for being in the house don't tell Karen I let you in, Okay?" Furlee meowed at him again and he patted her and poured some milk in her saucer. "Good night, Furlee."

"Meow," she said.

He walked out of the kitchen toward the sun-porch heading for Curt's room upstairs. His senses were supercharged with feelings of tenderness, joy, and love from seeing old friends, the holidays, and finding Virginia. The house was completely dark, and he could still smell the heavy floral odor of the gardenia and chrysanthemum Christmas arrangements set out for the party. Sweet cinnamon and allspice potpourri were mixed with the tart smell of evergreen from the fourteen-foot-tall Christmas tree, still glowing gaily and brightly with its beautiful ornaments and tiny white twinkling lights illuminating the brightly decorated presents under the tree's sloping limbs. The tree had the appearance of being covered with frozen crystallized icicles, and the reflected lights danced along the shadowed walls and black marbled fireplaces.

As Johnny reached out to open the stairwell door it clicked and swung open slowly by itself. In slow motion, it creaked as if in pain. Johnny froze in his steps with his hand still reaching out waiting to see who would come through the door. No one was there. The hair on his neck stood on end. He walked up the completely dark stairwell holding on to the handrail. He could hear his pulse beating in his ears as the steps on the stairs each made their individual groans, reporting their burden, one at a time.

He found his bed by the window of Curt's room, the window overlooking the magnolia tree, and looked out as the sun broke over the horizon. He started the timer on his wristwatch and thought about how lucky Karen and her family were to live in such a beautiful community and in such a wonderful home. It saddened him to think that he might not be able to spend much time here in the future, or with Virginia, if he took the lottery money and moved to Belize. Just as the sun cleared the horizon, he stopped the timer on his watch, it read two minutes and forty-three seconds.

SLEEPLESS

Johnny's Harley Davidson sat collecting dust under a blue canvas cover. An old discarded bimini top salvaged from a boat hid the motorcycle from the weather. Mid-April arrived and he still hadn't told Pim or Rocco whether or not he was riding with them to Taos, New Mexico, nor had he collected the lottery money.

Johnny had twice promised God that he would dedicate his life along with the lottery money in an effort to make the world a better place. But trying to come up with a realistic plan had become a major roadblock to Johnny. Procrastination had become the order of the day as Johnny waited with increasing impatience for some Divine inspiration.

Dan Rice had arranged for Johnny's dual citizenship and an incorporated tax shelter in Belize under the name of "Dream Machine, Inc." As soon as the IRS approved his nonprofit status nothing would be holding Johnny back from collecting the money.

Johnny wondered how often he would be allowed back into the United States when he left for Belize. He wondered if he would be allowed back in the United States to visit friends and relatives. He wondered if it was a good idea to avoid paying income taxes, even legally, if it meant giving up life in the United States. It seemed now like a good idea to make the motorcycle trip, his last stateside pleasure before he went off on the adventure of putting the lottery money to use. Becoming a one percenter, a multimillionaire, was on the horizon. He was nearly there. The motorcycle trip would allow him a little more time to consider everything.

Johnny called Rocco at work to discuss the departure date and trip details. He needed to make sure he was still invited, just as he had hoped, Rocco insisted that Johnny should join them.

"You only live once," Rocco said and he lamented that it was a short life, too. Johnny agreed. At this stage in life, his days were limited. The headiness of youth and a young man's myth of immortality had long ago disappeared.

Johnny called Virginia as soon as he had gotten off the telephone with Rocco, to see if she'd changed her mind about coming along. She wasn't home so he left a detailed message on her answering machine.

"Hey, Virginia, this is Johnny sorry I haven't call in a while. I just wanted you to know the trip to Taos is coming up. If you don't mind, I'd like to know how to get in touch with your friend. Okay, I, uh, guess I'll see you later. Bye." He hung up the telephone and sighed. He missed her, a lot. Virginia had taken several weeks to return his calls. He had called several times and figured her husband must have recovered. He tried to be happy for her when he thought of them together. He hadn't seen her since Christmas and when she finally did return his calls it was May 1st. She said she didn't know if her mother could watch Naichie for her or if she could arrange vacation to go along, but she would at least try to get word to White Deer that Johnny, and his friends were coming.

Johnny gave her a definite departure date and complete trip details. Although not much about the trip was written in stone. Johnny told Virginia everything, just in case she did make it. All she had to do was show up. Johnny coaxed her along as much as he could. He really hoped she would show up.

In the last few days Johnny had shopped in Covington several times, buying last minute camping and travel supplies. He went once to see

Leslie at the House of Travel in Baton Rouge to get whatever information she could provide on the area they expected to be traveling. The last day before the trip he went to work at the chemical plant wondering if he should give his resignation or wait until the lottery money hit the bank. He decided that it would be irresponsible to quit his job until he had money in the bank and told people at work only of the bike trip.

At last the long days of preparation were over and the evening of May 9th finally came around. He drove home from work on his motorcycle. For the last week he had been riding it everywhere he went wanting to make sure his riding muscles were somewhat in shape, and that the bike was in good working order.

That last night on his boat he spent reminiscing about motorcycle days of his past in the kerosene lamp light. Sleep was elusive as his mind raced with last minute details and excitement. He opened a bottle of red wine to ease his restless nerves, and wrote in his diary until near midnight.

Dear Diary

Something about my Harley Davidson FXRSP Low Rider kept breaking into my thoughts all week long. It seems very much like what draws people to sports—not just football, baseball, or golf, but more similar to hunting and fishing or horseback riding, too.

The first time my father, Johnny, Jr., took me for a spin, I was five years of age. We rode without helmets as there were no helmet laws in those days. The ride gave me a feeling of a freedom and excitement that wasn't expressible in my childish vocabulary. A bond of unbreakable friendship was formed between my Dad, and me during those summer afternoons.

We rode through the streets over to the neighborhood elementary school. Stopping on the baseball field's home plate, he put my hands on the handlebars.

"You steer it," he said. I attempted to steer it around first base as we went down the base line. I was unable to, or too fearful to.

"I can't do it," I said. So my father gently helped me to succeed in my first steering attempt on his vintage blue Harley 45. It was called a 45 because that was the cubic inches of engine piston displacement and it is the equivalent of today's Sporty.

Often, at home at night in front of the TV, my father would tell me stories of his early days, before I was born or before he'd gotten married. I would sit in his lap, snuggled and safe, and he would light up a filter less cigarette, sip his beer with salt poured by the triangular church key opening.

The aroma of the cigarette smoke and the beer would mingle with his words as he laughed and unrolled the dramas. The black and white television flickered somewhere in the back-ground, playing second fiddle to the storyteller and his son.

"Once Veron and his brother and I." My Dad began.

Veron and his brother were well-known characters to me. Though I had never met them, In my imagination they lived and breathed and were of legendary proportions. Veron had grown up to be a State Police officer, riding motorcycles on the highways catching speeders and criminals. His brother found some lesser job in my childish eyes, and therefore his occupation has slipped my memory. But I believe it was something of an owner of a grocery store.

"We were racing across this farm field," my father said. "And Veron was leading when suddenly the trail narrowed to a single plank across a wide ditch. Veron not wanting to lose his lead made a quick decision to chance the board."

I sat frozen, my eyes wide in suspense knowing Veron couldn't have made it across, the smile on my father's face told me so.

Breathless I asked, "Did he get hurt?"

"Well, Veron's bike made it halfway across," he said. "Before the board broke from the weight of his Electra Glide. Veron's brother and I stopped at the side of the ditch and laughed until we had to put our kickstands down or we would have fallen over."

"What kind of motorcycle did you have then?" I asked my father.

"An old 74," Johnny, Jr., replied.

"I wished you still had it, Dad," I had remembered saying.

It hadn't been hard for Rocco and Pim to convince Johnny to take the motorcycle trip west to Taos, New Mexico. They all would get a break from their daily routines and would ride across a lot of America he'd never before seen. Maybe he would even get to meet with the Medicine Man Virginia had told him about.

Of the bikers Pim and Rocco had hoped would come along, only Johnny agreed to depart on May 10, for "Discover America One," as Pim had titled the trip. Most of the bike riders Rocco and Pim knew were married and their wives didn't want their husbands riding off any great distances or lengths of time without them.

The adventurers agreed to meet at Pot of Gold, a classic Louisiana gambling truck stop with the legal maximum limit of fifty video poker machines, a greasy spoon 24-hour restaurant to attract potential gamblers after regular bars closed down, a service station that was open 24 hours a day, and a parking lot big enough to hold an 18-wheeler convention. The pot holes were large enough to lose a small car in.

This spot was good for several reasons, it would be open when they arrived at 6:00 in the morning, they could fill their gas tanks and drink a cup of hot coffee, hopefully fresh, and, most importantly, it sat at the entrance to the old highway they had chosen for departing the city of Baton Rouge.

GOING, GOING GONE

It was a restless night, getting to bed late after cleaning and stowing away everything on the boat. Finishing the last minute packing and checking off his trip supply list had taken much longer than he had planned. Then he added a few optional items in his waterproof travel bag, until it could hardly hold anything else. Johnny tried to ignore an uneasy feeling in the pit of his stomach. Somehow, he knew his life would never be the same.

Bad weather had delayed the "Discover America One" departure for days and it hadn't improved this evening, but Johnny had decided as he went to sleep, he would go no matter what the out come of the weather, whether or not the others were going. Virginia hadn't called to confirm or decline, so she was certainly out of the trip. Even if he traveled alone, he was going on this trip.

Finally, almost as a relief, the alarm sounded, he felt he'd only been asleep a couple hours. He swung his legs out of the berth, found the floor and reached for the cabin light. The bright fluorescent light was too much for his sleep-deprived eyes, so he flipped it back off and turned on the red navigation light. The red light was designed to keep a mariner's eyes from losing their night vision ability during night passages. It was a feature Johnny rarely used.

Stumbling around in the red glow he took a shower and dressed in the clothes he'd laid out the night before. Gathering his bags, he set them out on the wooden dock, damp from the dew, and checked his trip departure list one more time.

Taking one more look around, he checked to be sure all the hatches were closed, all the vents were opened, and all the electrical switches were off except for the battery charger and the bilge pumps. At last satisfied he could do no more, he climbed out to the stern and locked the combination lock on the door hasp. He hadn't told anyone other than Virginia he was really leaving, and he hope no one would miss him. He hadn't heard from Karen or Lee in a few weeks and now he would be out of beeper range. He made a mental note to call them later, during the trip.

Johnny carried his gear along the floating dock to the parking lot. The dock squeaked and rattled under the combined weight of his bags and him. His bike was wet from rains that passed through during the night. He'd left it uncovered yesterday after returning from work. He laid his hand flat on the black leather seat and swept off the big pools of rainwater that had accumulated during the night.

Johnny made several attempts to fasten his bag in the most efficient way, a feat he failed to engineer before this morning. He settled on a compromise that included six bungee cords. Six was all he had. He could have used less but nervous energy was driving him to procrastinate and tinker.

All three of the guys going on the trip had discussed the needed gear and clothes several times on the telephone over the last few days. At first, the general thinking had been that they could share some common needs, like tools and fix-a-flat aerosol cans. It would reduce their individual loads, they thought. But in the end, Johnny had insisted on being completely self-sufficient. Finally, he threw his leg over the bike, sitting on the damp seat. He leaned against his travel bag to see if he'd mounted it forward enough to give him good back support. He decided that it could be pushed further forward, but he would make those adjustments later.

As the remaining night's rain soaked through his freshly washed blue jeans, it seemed to him that the bike and he were fusing, becoming a team, half white-buffalo and half man.

Across the long concrete bridge leading into the marina's island parking lot, a car's headlights pierced the darkness through the thick slow-moving morning fog. He wondered who would be coming to the marina this late at night or early in the morning. He watched as the car halted in a parking space next to him.

When the automobile's lights went off, he could see Virginia's sleepy face through the windshield as she opened the door and she stepped out. She walked over carrying a large backpack in one hand and a sleeping bag in the other. She was wearing blue jeans, a long sleeve work shirt, and boots. He looked at her moving toward him, amazed that he could have forgotten how beautiful she was.

"JT, I thought you might not mind if I come along after all," she said. She was shocked to see Johnny on his motorcycle, and was impressed with how awake he looked.

"No, Virginia, I wouldn't mind at all," he said. "I was hoping you would come. You almost missed me though, I'm ready to leave now. Do you need anything else?" He was shocked at her sudden appearance and climbed off the bike wondering how he could attach her bags and still have room for both of them to sit.

"No, I ate some fruit on the drive over, and I have two changes of clothes in my back pack," She said. Standing there smiling from ear to ear, Johnny leaned over and gave her a warm hug. Their bodies fit together perfectly as if they had been made for each other. Johnny gave her a kiss on her cheek. He couldn't be sure but he thought he heard her gasp as he released her. He began by taking the budgies cords off his bag, then reloaded both their bags and sleeping bags. This time with Virginia's help the process seemed simpler than before.

"Okay, here's your first lesson," he said. "Always mount from the left side, just like a horse," he said. Virginia did as instructed, lifting her long leg with grace and ease and settled behind Johnny. She'd ridden many times behind Michael but decided not to mention that.

"This passenger seat is really soft," she said. Johnny didn't know if she was joking or not, but there was nothing he could do about it anyway at this point in their journey. Reaching into his pocket, he pulled out his key chain. In the darkness, he couldn't easily tell the bike's key from the others, so he fumbled around in the fluorescent marina lighting, looking at their silhouettes, he finally spied the bike's ignition key. His fingers grasp it between the thumb and forefinger, and then slipped it into the bike's switch on the steering column. He felt each of the lock's tumblers slipping over the keyed edges until it settled in and bottomed out with a crisp snap. This was the moment where Johnny usually got excited about riding his bike. This meant that all plans and preparations were complete, and all the bikes systems were checked and in working order. He raised the bike off its kickstand, tilting the weight of the three of them straight up and asked Virginia if she was ready.

"Yeah, ready and, God willing, able," she said. Common sense had told her not to even consider going on this trip. She knew Naichie would love spending time with his grandmother. Michael was being taken care of, as good as worldly possible in the nursing home. She not only had work covered, but her mother and her employer both had encouraged her to go. Virginia had become a workaholic since Michael had gone into the nursing home. She could hardly stand being home in the evenings or even on weekends. If it hadn't been for Naichie, Virginia wasn't sure what would have happened to her.

Johnny twisted the key in a clockwise movement, the headlight lit up, boring a passageway through the darkness across the white shell parking lot and down the bridge. A mist of fog drifted around them, hypnotically swirling across the Harley Davidson's beam of light.

Johnny pulled out the choke, flicked the throttle half way, and pushed the starter button on the FXRSP.

Johnny's Harley Davidson was a police bike he had picked up in Houston, Texas, back in 1992. He had originally ordered a bike from a Harley Davidson dealership in New Orleans in 1992. Month after month, he had waited, checking with the shop, thinking that any day he would get word on his bike's arrival.

Finally after a year of waiting he'd been told there was no hope of getting a new police bike. So, he began to call Harley Davidson shops around the Gulf Coast hoping to find one somewhere. Even in 1992 there had been a waiting list. Finally when he called a Harley dealer in Houston the salesperson, whose name was Gritt, told Johnny they had a police demo with a little over 10,000 miles on it.

"Yeah, we've got a police demo," Gritt said.

"How much do you want for it?" Johnny said.

"Eight thousand bucks," Gritt said. "It's still under warranty."

He asked Gritt if he would accept a credit card number over the phone to purchase it, or at least hold it until he could get a look at it.

"I'll hold it for you till we open tomorrow," Gritt said. Johnny called to cancel his plans for the next day and had a restless sleep that night.

He'd left the boat at 3:00 A.M. and drove the 350-miles in a pickup truck he owned at the time. He arrived at little before 9:00 A.M., as the shop was opening. Gritt, the sales clerk he had spoken to the day before, showed him the FXRSP and Johnny was ecstatic. Big, powerful, and white the handlebars looked like chromed horns. The second Johnny saw it he knew it would always be a white buffalo to him. However, Gritt refused to let him test ride it after Johnny admitted he didn't have a motorcycle endorsement on his driver's license.

"Son, you can't test drive the damn thing if you don't have a motorcycle endorsement on your drivers license," Gritt said.

Johnny told Gritt about his father's old bikes and how his brother would often let him ride his Wide Glide. Finally to shut him up, Gritt told Johnny to pick out a helmet and gave him the FXR's key.

"Go up the interstate entrance ramp at the end of this parking lot," Gritt said. "Go down two exits west on the 610 Loop and then come back." Johnny climbed on the bike and started it.

"What's the gear shift pattern?" Johnny asked. "One down three up?" Gritt looked at Johnny with regret in his eyes, nodding yes. Johnny let out the clutch and the bike nearly left him sitting in the parking lot. An adrenaline rush enabled him to barely regain control before he ran out into the highway service road.

He didn't want Gritt to suspect that his instinct to refuse Johnny the test drive been a good hunch. So Johnny leaned forward in the saddle and twisted the throttle open again directing the bike up the 610-entrance ramp. As he reached the top of the ramp, catching a glimpse of the heavy seven-lanes of traffic, he realized for the second time in fifteen seconds that he had no business test driving this motorcycle here. It would have been much wiser to take it home to test drive. After all it was still under factory-warranty.

He shifted the bike up into second gear and twisted the throttle again. Fear turned his knuckles white as he squeezed the handle grips and the bike roared out into the seven lanes of 85-mph morning rush hour traffic. He fought for his life in the bumper to bumper madness, twisting the throttle and shifting instinctively trying to obtain the same speed as the charging mass of Detroit steel that was barreling down on him from all sides.

Just about the time he reached a communal speed with the wild tangle of traffic, the bike's engine started violently missing. At that moment, Johnny's life passed before his eyes. Seeing an exit sign passing over his head, he made an immediate right turn off the Loop and went down the exit ramp. Managing to slow down enough he followed the turnaround going back under the highway and was headed back up onto the Interstate 610 Loop, back in the direction of the dealership.

As he coasted along in the turnaround, he noticed the engine had smoothed out and seemed to be operating normally. Even so, he looked around for some safer way to get back, nothing looked obvious. The neighborhoods appeared uninviting and he couldn't be sure if any of them were through streets back to the dealership.

Looking around quickly he made up his mind to try to get back on the 610 Loop and accelerated full throttle, back up the ramp. He shot up into the mad rush of morning traffic, leaning into the wind. Out into the Kamikaze traffic at 80 mph as if propelled by a sling shot and again the Harley began to vibrate and miss violently. Shifting into 4th gear the motor smoothed out and he made a mental note to have the dealership check into the engine miss as soon as he got back. If the bike and he made it back.

Gritt the salesman was waiting for him out in the parking lot. He had heard the bike coming back down the interstate off ramp. When Johnny pulled up to the front door and took the too small helmet off his head, his smile had disappeared.

"It's got a bad high speed miss," he said. Gritt looked at him with an expression that made Johnny want to crawl under the helmet.

"You forgot to shift up," Gritt smirked.

"What?" Johnny said.

"That's the high RPM limiter—it kicks in at 6200 and cuts the engine out," Gritt said. "So you won't blow her up."

"Oh, I see. Sorry about that," Johnny said. "I'll take the bike if you'll accept an out-of-town check or a Visa Card?" He handed the keys back to Gritt.

"We'll have to take the police lights off—it's against the law for you to ride with police lights," informed Gritt.

"Do you have a ramp to get it in the back of my truck?" Johnny asked. Everything he said sounded so stupid as it came out of his mouth. There was definitely a personality conflict going on here, Johnny felt.

"Yeah, guy, let me see your drivers license." Gritt mumbled something else and walked away looking annoyed. Johnny felt like a greenhorn nerd.

"You know my father used to ride," he said. But Gritt didn't look back.

The predawn marina parking lot exploded with Harley muffler noise as Johnny pushed the kickstand up and let out the clutch. Virginia and he slipped off into the early morning fog, bike rumbling away from the dock. The white mud shell parking lot made squishing noises at little more than idle speed.

"Speak now or for two weeks hold your peace," he said. Virginia didn't answer.

The sun wouldn't be up for another couple of hours and the predawn fog was thick and wet on their faces. It soaked into their clothes and skin as they rode. Gracefully they swung the bike into a low left turn and headed west on Highway 22. Getting the feel of each other's balance was coming quickly to both of them. The bike, loaded with baggage and two people, handled well as they crossed over the swing bridge's metal grating over the Tchefuncta River. They slipped as quietly as possible into the ancient sleeping village of Madisonville, once called Cocodrie, meaning oyster shells, by the early French settlers and Indians. Not wanting to wake a person or barking dog, they coasted along speechless in the dark night.

Finally as they crept away from town, Johnny began to open up on the throttle and soon they were roaring through the darkness. The wet country roads hissed as the tires parted the puddles, and a feeling that something very big was happening to them began settling into their stomachs. They each slipped into their own thoughts, meditating privately far away from where they were, at that moment. And at the same time they grew comfortable leaning against each other and appreciative of the warmth of their combined bodies.

They pulled into the Pot of Gold truck stop, on the outskirts of Baton Rouge about an hour later. Their bodies vibrating from the motor cycle, It had been anticlimactic to stop so soon on such a long journey. Pim and Rocco hadn't arrived yet, so Johnny and Virginia topped off the bikes gas tank and went inside to get a cup of hot coffee. They were talking to the nearly toothless cashier and sipping hot coffee when Pim pulled up to the gas pumps first, Rocco idled in right behind him and the cashier turned to see the other two bikes.

"Where y'all headed?" the cashier said. Johnny was in the middle of a yawn, he wished now he could have gotten more sleep.

"Out West, to Taos New Mexico," Virginia replied. "We're going to visit a friend of mine."

"Never been west of Texas myself," the cashier said.

Rocco and Pim came in to pay for their gas and got a cup of coffee.

"You want to eat breakfast now or wait for another gas stop down the road?" Pim asked. They looked at Virginia curiously, with out saying a word as they sipped their coffee. Johnny had not mentioned her to them.

"Hey, guys, this is Virginia. Virginia, this is Pim and Rocco," Johnny said. "I hope you don't mind if she comes along?" They looked at Virginia, then at Johnny, then at each other, then back to Johnny.

"No, we don't mind if she comes along as long as she's got an iron butt and a strong bladder," Rocco said. "We don't like making too many pit stops." Rocco smiled at Virginia.

"Rocco, I'll bet you I can sit on the back of Johnny's bike a lot longer than you can drive your bike," she said as she smiled defiantly.

"Y'all hungry?" Pim said. Pim was the diplomat of the two, always trying to make peace where Rocco enjoyed stirring up trouble, although more as a practical joker and never meaning to cause any real problems.

"We'll pass," Johnny said, "We're too pumped up to eat just yet. Looks like we might get some more rain. If you're ready, let's go on." The sun was making an effort to show it self but clouds covered the horizon.

They walked back out to their bikes by the gas pumps. Rocco hopped on his bike and pulled out of the parking lot first, first for the last time on the trip. Morning traffic was already starting to build as they rode west down rough old Highway 190.

"Virginia, are you comfortable back there?" Johnny said. He had to yell over the roar of the bike's exhaust and the tires on the highway. Virginia leaned in closer to Johnny's ear and their helmets bumped together as they dipped through one of the many potholes.

"I'm fine," she said. Her voice was raised and high pitched and cut through all the low dull road noises and vibrations. "Thanks for the ear plugs."

"No problem," Johnny yelled back over his shoulder, the wind and the forward movement of the bike help deliver his words to her ears, though his deeper voice did tend to get lost in the roar of the bikes engine. They crossed the Mississippi River, looking out over it from great advantage in the air. They could feel the air turn cooler over the wide muddy expanse of water and could see miles of river winding upstream toward the northwest.

The bridge pilings acted as a manmade river roadblock to large ocean-going vessels. Huey P. Long, as Governor of the State of Louisiana had built the bridge in a fashion that prevented access to ports north of Baton Rouge. Johnny thought of Tom Sawyer, Huck Finn, and river rafts as he watched the swirling Mississippi River currents tossing trees like twigs around in the muddy water far below.

Before they'd burned half the first tank of gas, the rain began to fall in earnest. The four of them pulled over to put on their rain suits in the little town of Port Berry. A convenience store gas station offered a protective roof from the weather and Johnny and Virginia stood watching, as the rain grew stronger. Virginia reached into her raincoat pocket and pulled out a cigarette lighting it while Pim and Rocco walked into the store. Johnny had never seen her smoke before.

"Virginia, that smells wonderful," he said. "What kind of cigarette is that?"

"American Spirit," she said. "They have no additives, just tobacco. Most brands add things to the tobacco to help it burn faster, taste different, I don't know exactly what but it's not natural I'm sure."

"I've never seen those before," he said. "Actually I've never seen you smoke before."

"You can find them at tobacco shops," she said. "I don't smoke often, I bought these for the trip."

"May I try one of those?" he asked. Virginia pulled one out and handed it to him. He leaned over as Virginia took her lighter from her pocket. Striking it, she held the flame steady for him as he pulled off of it. A long first drag coated his lungs with the thick nicotine laden smoke. He breathed it out slowly as the rain quickened wind pulled it away from his lips.

"I had forgotten how these things taste," he said. Taking another drag the thick smoke exited from his nose and mouth as he spoke. Virginia looked at Johnny unbelievingly.

"I haven't smoked a cigarette in years," he said. "I've only smelled the aroma of other people's cigarettes." Virginia shook her head at Johnny.

"I wouldn't have given you one if I had known that," she said in disgust.

"Virginia, you really shocked the hell out of me this morning," he said, "when you showed up at the marina. Another minute and I would have been gone."

"JT, I know you didn't expect me, and if you really don't want me here, I can get home?" she said. "I'm a big girl."

"No, Virginia," he said. "That's not it at all, I'm glad you're here, I hope you are glad you're here too. This is going to be one of those adventures we can think about when we get too old to have any more adventures."

"I couldn't sleep last night wondering why you wanted to visit White Deer?" she said.

"I can't tell you everything, Virginia-not yet," he said. "There are a lot of things going on in my life. I need to find some answers."

"JT, you said you were Catholic," she said. He nodded his head. "Have you spoken to anyone in your church?" he nodded again.

"I believe there are things in this world that urgently need to be resolved," he said. "I really believe the world is suffering from Easter Island disease." He laughed at his diagnosis. "If we don't start working to control humankind's consumption of natural resources, we're doomed. My local priest advises that I concern myself with only those things that I have control over. That's a huge question all in itself. What do we have control over? Was it okay for the Catholic Church to ignore the Holocaust? I think not. I've been trying to draw those lines all my life. I keep hearing that this could be the end times. There are many things prophesied, that have come to pass." Johnny was hoping he didn't sound like some crazy doom's dayer.

"Like what?" she asked.

"Well, Christian faiths of all denominations," he said. "They're saying that according to the Bible the world has come to the end-times. The Jewish people have some kind of a prophecy of end times that has recently revealed itself. Tibetan monks have a seventeen hundred-year-old prophecy that calls on the Red Man to take over the spirituality of the world. Something like "When the bird flies on wings of iron, when the horse runs on legs of iron," and something else I forget. But when these things come to pass their ancient spiritual leader prophesied that the Red Man would take over the spiritual leadership of the world. They say that those signs have come to pass."

"Damn, Virginia, seventeen hundred years ago no one had discovered America yet," he said. "Let alone the Red Man, as for as I know anyway. Then, the Catholic Church has some millennial prediction that parallels the American Indian White Buffalo vision you and I talked about the night we met in Gulf Shores."

"I didn't know the Catholics had a millennial prediction?" Virginia asked.

"Yeah, I heard it last year," he said. "Something about Satan being cast into Hell for a thousand years, the people of the earth living without sin. It's part of that end times stuff going around.

"I'm not saying that I believe the world is doomed in the near future," he said. "But I do believe a turning point has come, and it's time for the world's peoples to recognize that spirituality is the reason to get up in the morning. Not how many material possessions we can accumulate before we die. Or how prestigious a job or life we can have. Or even how can we survive one more day."

"Hey, JT, y'all ready to go?" Rocco said. He and Pim walked out to their bikes. Virginia and Johnny tossed their cigarettes into an ashtray by the no smoking sign at the store's entrance.

"Let's get this show on the road, we're burning daylight," she said. Johnny laughed at her gig at Rocco.

THE ROAD OF NO RETURN

Pim rode a 1987 Low Rider Harley Davidson with nearly 50,000 miles on it, Rocco had owned it before Pim. The bike had been some shade of red before Rocco had it custom repainted one of those enamel colors that changed in different lighting.

Pim was a little taller than average height and his strength of character made up for any shortcomings he may have had as a person. He was an easy person to be around who liked to have fun and take chances. His bike was usually the first to pull out of the parking lot. Rocco wasn't in a hurry very often. Rocco, slipped his sunglasses on his broad sun tanned face, turned to Virginia, and smiled.

"Hey Virginia, you sure you're up for this trip?" Rocco asked.

"I still say I can sit back here a lot longer than you can steer that thing," she said. Virginia pulled her face shield down over her helmet and leaned back against the sissy bar. Johnny slid his WWI pilot's goggles on and then his helmet. He was still thinking about his conversation with Virginia.

"Virginia," he yelled over his shoulder. "Do you get the feeling that our lives aren't going to be the same after this trip?" Virginia leaned in against Johnny's back to make sure she could hear him over the motorcycle engines.

"You mean like for us personally?" she said.

"Yeah, that," he said. "But I get this feeling that you and I are riding to destiny not a destination," he said.

"I can hardly hear what you're saying, JT," she said. "Hold that thought until we stop again." Johnny pulled out of the parking lot of the gas station behind Rocco.

There was heavy 18-wheeler truck traffic on the old two-lane, pot holed black top road. It was hard staying in a single lane when a truck passed by going the opposite direction. This road had been the main route for east-west travel in Louisiana until the Interstate 10 was constructed after World War II.

Since Highway 190 was a secondary road now, it wasn't kept up as it had been in years gone by. Parts of Highway 190 had been in use since the Spanish Conquistadors had ruled the region. Parts of it were still occasionally referred to as the Old Spanish Trail. Nowadays it was Louisiana's equivalent of the old Route 66 that went across America out West.

The four riders passed through tiny Louisiana French communities like Opelousas, where Jim Bowie once lived and Eunice. Breakfast smells were in the air as the tiny village got their children off to school.

An ancient form of provincial French was still commonly spoken in these areas, though much more rarely these days than just a generation ago. The people of the small towns turned to watch the bikes as they idled by. Virginia felt like she was riding in a parade and wished for beads or throws to toss to the children, especially the little boys who watched open jawed as the throbbing Harleys cruised along.

Time was slowly pulling these small farming communities into the modern economy of the information age. However, as long as their agricultural world was still needed to feed the people in the larger cities they would survive a little longer quietly huddled in their shrinking economies. Their French language and culture were slowly evaporating to the heat of televisions, internet screens, and schools designed to turn out industrial age factory workers.

"Turn up here," Rocco signaled. He was the self-appointed keeper of the map. "Follow me," he said. He roared past the other two bikes and turned right by a towering gray galvanized rice drier. Farmers brought harvested rice crops there to be dried and prepared for shipping, a couple of miles east of the small town of Elton. Pim sped his bike up to catch Rocco, leaving Virginia and Johnny in the rear of the yuppie motorcycle gang. Johnny glanced in his rear view mirror and noticed a white car. The car turned on the road behind them, following at a distance. Freshly planted farm fields lined the road on both sides of the rutted black top. Weathered wooden equipment sheds dotted the landscapes, leaning bravely against the elements, relics from long forgotten struggles. Years ago Johnny's grandfather had worked as a sharecropper near there, after losing his rice drier business during the Great Depression.

"Why are you letting Rocco and Pim get so far ahead of us?" Virginia asked. Johnny glanced into his rear view mirror again.

"There is a car about a half a mile behind us," he said. "It might be an unmarked police car." She leaned forward to see the car in the motorcycle's rear view mirror.

"What makes you believe that the car behind us is a law enforcement officer?" she asked.

"Really just a hunch, but he is maintaining an equal distance" he said. Johnny looked at the speedometer and increased the motorcycle's speed two miles over the speed limit in an effort to catch up with the other bikes. Minutes later they arrived in the tiny town of Oberlin, Louisiana.

Johnny and Virginia rolled into a gas station where Rocco and Pim had already dismounted and were in the process of taking off their helmets and rain gear.

"JT, why did you stay so far behind us?" Pim asked. Just then, an unmarked police car pulled slowly up into the gas station parking lot, beside the motorcycles.

"You boys were driving just a little over the speed limit back there," he said. The four motorcycle riders stared at the officer not knowing what to say. "Y'all aren't planning on staying around here are y'all?"

"No, sir, just getting a little gas and passing through," Rocco said. The police officer looked at them, considering what he would do next.

"I don't want to see y'all around here speeding again," the officer said. He took his gaze off them and pulled out of the parking lot. Johnny gave a friendly wave toward the police car as it drove away.

"That's why I didn't catch up with you guys," he said.

"Oh, crap," said Rocco. "That was close. We haven't made it out of Louisiana yet and the cops are chasing us." They stretched their legs and filled the bikes with gas at the self-service pump. A station attendant walked out to look at the bikes, waiting to collect their money.

"Where you guys headed?" he asked. He was standing in front of Rocco's bike. Pim looked up.

"Taos, New Mexico," Pim replied.

"Oh, man, y'all surely have a long way to go," the attendant said. "My name's Earl. One day I'd like to do that, you know, get on a Harley Davidson and get a glimpse of America before we become a third world country."

"Third world country? What do you mean by that?" Pim asked.

"Well you know, the shape of our politics in Washington," Earl said. "Multinational companies are running this country. The elections are no more than auctions of political power. Highest bidder takes all."

"Never heard it explained so simply," Virginia replied. "So how does that make us a third world country?" The station attendant studied them, wondering if it was safe to continue his dissertation. He straightened his ragged cap, placing it back on his head with the brim pointed nearly straight up.

"Appears to me," Earl said, putting his hands in his pockets after looking at his dirty finger nails. "that until we get special interest out of the political system our elected officials are going to continue to give away the wealth and natural resources of America to the highest bidder."

"What do you mean politicians are giving away America's wealth?" Rocco asked. Rocco had been trying to ignore him the best he could but that got his attention. Rocco generally didn't trust strangers, especially ones that weren't members of his political party.

"It's really simple," Earl said. "They're doing it right in front of our faces. Special interest groups, multinational companies, even foreign countries. Hell anyone with big money that contributes to the election campaign of a candidate or political party. The candidates then are obliged to give them something in return. You know, scratch my back, I'll scratch yours. The "good old boys" kind of thing. The President of the good ole United States has taken money from communist and dictators and God only knows who else and in return gave away things like fighter plane, rocket and missile technology."

Earl just wouldn't quit. Johnny was wondering if he could change the subject before Rocco got really upset. They all finished filling their gas tanks and followed Earl into the tiny office to the cash register.

"We didn't even share that technology with our allies," Earl went on. "It's a free-for-all up there, free for everyone but the American citizen. We're paying billions for the creation of the technology that's vital to our country's defense, and for a few hundred thousand or a million dollars our politicians give it away. Giving it away to a communist country that doesn't even recognize basic human rights."

"Hell," Earl said. "Did you know they dissect their living death row inmates in the prisons and sell their organs one at a time to wealthy people who need transplants?"

"We'd better get a move on toward Taos, New Mexico, Earl," Rocco said. Earl returned their credit cards, and they signed for the gas.

"You know the Pope is even saying that globalization by the super-wealthy is creating huge gaps between the rich and poor," Earl said. "I saw him on TV the other day telling the powers-that-be that they must make a better effort to take care of the poverty-stricken masses." The motorcycle riders walked back to their bikes with Earl still talking by the cash register.

"Made a lot of sense," Johnny said. The sun was heating up, causing heat waves to dance across the sticky black top road in the distance.

"Yeah, but he's crazy," Rocco said.

"What he's saying is really the truth, and too close for comfort," Virginia said.

They rolled up their rain suits and stuck them on the outside of their bags under the bungee cords. That way the rain suits would have a chance to dry and wouldn't smear road film on their clean clothes inside of the travel bags. Pim was the first again to pull out of the service station and he waved back at Earl as he drove away.

The four of them rode as hard as the road conditions, speed limits, and traffic would allow. About lunchtime, Rocco led them to a small restaurant in the small town of Jasper, just inside of the Texas border. The restaurant belonged to Rocco's cousin. Being the navigator for the road trip. Rocco had conveniently routed them to visit his brother-in-law, in Alexandria, Louisiana, earlier in the day and now they would visit cousin Sam in Jasper, Texas.

The restaurant was a little Depression Era Tex-Mex food place right next door to a small motel of the same era. Cousin Sam owned both places. Virginia slipped off the bike first, as usual, so that Johnny could swing his leg over the seat easier.

"How do you feel?" she asked.

"I feel fine," Johnny said. Virginia unbuckled her helmet.

"Hey, guys, Rocco and I want to eat," Pim said. "Are y'all coming in?"

"Yeah," Johnny said. Rocco and Pim walked inside the restaurant, with Virginia and Johnny following.

Cousin Sam's restaurant had a unique arrangement, several long wooden picnic-style tables in the smoke filled dining room. The lunch crowd was still eating and everybody who was anybody in Jasper was there. Cousin Sam sat the four bike riders down at a table that could have been twenty feet long.

The town doctor, a state policeman, and the mayor sat across from Richard Redhead, a California senator who was in town for his wife's family reunion. They sat gossiping about politics and swapping insults, each trying to impress the other with their superior grasp of National politics.

Johnny decided that trading insults must be a local custom. Rocco's Cousin Sam, a big barrel chested, pot bellied, Texas macho sort of man who always had the right thing to say, introduced everyone. The waiter came over and introduced herself. She was a fifty-something, Yellow Rose of Texas sort of once-blond woman. She still kept up her figure and genuinely liked the people she waited on. She smiled largely while she helped them make their selections from the parchment paper menus stained with greasy fingerprints and dried Bar-B-Q sauce.

An old Catholic priest wearing the traditional black shirt, pants and shoes with the white color insert came through the front door and limped toward their table with his cane. He walked in a crooked deliberate maner, never taking a single step for granted. Occasionally lifting his hardly combed head of thick white hair, he peered up from a permanently bent posture making sure he was still heading in the right direction. His plump physique, and long over-grown bushy, gray eyebrows gave him the appearance of an over-stuffed toy.

"What will you have today, Padre', the usual?" Sam asked. Hunched over, the old man held firmly onto his cane with one hand while he paused. Lifting his head, he smiled a youthful grin to everyone in the room and nodded slightly to Sam. His stiff movements and tiny steps however showed he was very old. Working his way around the room, he sat directly across from Virginia and Johnny and stored his cane under the bench with a dull thump.

"Good afternoon Father," Johnny said. They were sitting eye to eye.

"Hello, son," the old priest replied. Johnny could not tell whether or not the Priest was interested in conversation. Not knowing anything about local politics and not wanting to chance an insult as seemed the local custom required, Johnny just smiled at the old man. The priest looked back with a mysterious gleam in his eye. The rest of the dinners were busy arguing, with food in their mouths, about the last local election. The mayor was apparently losing control of his temper, hammering his knife hard on the table. Dishes and silverware bounced each time he did.

"Why can't everybody just get along, Father?" Johnny asked. The old priest looked at Johnny and his eyes glazed over for a long moment. Apparently he was sizing Johnny up as he might do a congregation on any particular Sunday. After a while Johnny began to wonder if the priest might be dying and regretted that he'd asked the question. The priest still sat there with his head tilted slightly to one side staring into space in Johnny's general direction.

Panicking, Johnny looked around to see if anybody else was alarmed, but none of the locals seemed to have noticed anything wrong. Still he sat motionless, slightly hunched over, in his starched shirt and pants. The loose skin from his weathered chin completely covering his little white collar insert. Johnny wanted to jump out of his cow hide-covered chair and check the priest's pulse. He was sure the old fellow must be dying right in front of him. Everyone sat arguing oblivious to the emergency. Nobody noticing or doing anything to help.

Johnny worried that it had been his question that caused the priest' heart to stop beating. God, he hoped no one had been listening to their conversation. In his minds eye Johnny could see tomorrow's Jasper, Texas, newspaper "Catholic Priest dies from question asked by a motorcycle diner at Sam's Restaurant. Motorcycle-rider and female companion being held-pending charges of involuntary manslaughter."

To Johnny's relief the old Priest slowly began to straighten his grayed head and closed his partially opened mouth. Johnny was much joyed by this improvement and had lost his appetite but sat there speechlessly in expectation as the Priest began to talk.

"Each of us walks through life singularly, sometimes sharing a quiet time or an outing with a family member or a friend," said the priest. "We all contemplate life's purpose, hoping to bring order to chaos and meaning to our existence. Searching for signs along the highway of life, somehow we survive to proceed and progress."

Johnny looked around the table to see if anyone else was listening to the old priest. No one appeared to have even noticed that Father Charles was talking.

"Each decision we make," the priest continued. "Seemingly reveals the nature of God's creation in our own being. And if we are careful our personal expression of God's Creation comes together in a constructive way. Piece by piece our reflection appears in His-story.

"On life's winding road each one of us awakens, each in our own time, catching a glimpse of our role in the lineage of our personal family and that of our larger human family. We come to realize we are a genetic messenger from the past, a member of a lineage passed down through ages long forgotten. Parent to child genetic pools built by individuals selecting each other, going back into time immortal, handing down not only the baton of genetic accumulation but in the process of surviving passing along lessons from the family's existence," the old priest said.

"The knowledge of plants that heal, methods of food gathering and preparation, recipes, all fit together. Practice becomes method, method becomes culture, culture becomes tradition and tradition gives rise to ceremonies," Father Charles said.

"Only a few generations ago, communities were more isolated. Walking, riding cattle, or paddling boats were the only means of transportation. This geographically limited isolation kept cultures homogeneous. This oneness allowed societies to be congenial and individuals predictable. This communal uniformness allowed for specialized and sophisticated norms of behavior. The specialization of behavior provided guidelines in which to interact within the intimate society. Predicable interaction became the basis of a civilization," he spoke softly across the table and Johnny had forgotten where he was or that anyone was near by.

"That homogeneousness allowed for tight rules of interaction, mating customs, methods to raise children, and structure to provide for the needy. Proven through millenniums of human experience, etiquette becomes an outward reflection of the people and culture itself. In the past the world seemed much larger with cultures much smaller, more collective. First they were separated by geographical borders, then by religious differences or tenets of belief, then, later by political structure. Communities stretching back into prehistoric times shared not only a common existence and reality, but also similar genetic traits. For many thousands of years individual cultures have, of necessity specialized. Narrow gene structures reinforced by limited territories produced highly individualized gene pools, spiritual belief, knowledge bases, cultures, and political structures," the old priest said.

"Now," Father Charles said. "what happens when rapid mass communications and transportation shrinks the world into instant gratification? Who will be left standing when the dust settles from the inevitable disputes and power struggles? What will the people of the one world community believe in? Survival of the fittest would be the beginning of the end. Could fear and hate supersede kindness and congeniality? It mustn't," the priest admonished.

"Religious zealots of all different peoples will denounce the inevitable blending of religious doctrines as heresy. Believing in their particular spiritual and cultural mores must be heralded as the only way. Truly good leaders must search for a common ground or good.

"Political extremist will espouse as errors any systems their factions do not control. Nationalists will maintain their people's culture as superior. Like peoples will hail themselves master races."

"In spite of the well-meaning groups creation will frolic in the futile, egomaniac attempts of mankind to show a particular personal superiority. The secret to the survival of humanity lies in the complete and unconditional acceptance of their fellow humans. As the Bible instructs us, although few who read it really understand its message, until we truly love our neighbors as ourselves," Father Charles said and added, "Hate the sin, but love the sinner."

GENOCIDE IN THE GARDEN OF EDEN

"That sounds like that sermon you gave only last week, Padre," the state policeman said. "I think America is the best place to live on this here earth. If a person can't survive here, he'd probably die quicker anywhere else, anyhow. You think it's any accident that most of the people in the world are starving. Hell, no. Them poor foreigners don't believe in Jesus Christ or know how to run a democracy, that's why they're suffering."

Dick Redhead sat next to the state policeman nodding his head in agreement. Johnny sat still determand to stay out of the argument. He figured it was a local problem and there was no point in getting involved with something he couldn't do anything about.

"Why we were just talking in Bible study down at the church," the state policeman said, "that all the great modern world powers are Christian, that's why America's great, because this great country was founded on Christianity. Hell, the Founding Fathers of this great nation founded this great country on Christianity. That's what made America great." The state policeman stared straight at Virginia figuring she was some "wet-back" Mexican in the country illegally.

"That's a load of crap," Virginia said. She stood up pointing her finger into the stunned police officer's face. Johnny dropped his fork and stopped chewing, getting ready to grab her. The whole table went silent even the smiling waitress froze in her tracks.

"This great country, this great world power was founded on the death bed of the genocide of American Indians, the real owners of your America," she said. "But I guess since they weren't Christians it was okay to kill them, men, women and innocent children, and steal their land?" She looked as if she were about to leap over the table to get at the Texas State Policeman. He sat there shocked, mouth open, half-chewed food showing.

"Men, women, and children were systematically rounded up out of their homes, off their lands and headed off to worthless territory," she said. "Or even worse, killed, enslaved, lied to, and forgotten, over and over again, even in these modern times."

Senator Redhead made a mental note to find out who these people were. They sounded dangerous and talk like that couldn't be taken lightly.

"Even though they believed in One God," Virginia continued. "They were considered less than human. Truth is, America the beautiful, land of the free, home of the brave is a pack of lies. It's a saga of greed, domination, and genocide." Virginia was staring at the police officer, straight into his eyes, and neither one of them blinked. The police officer's hand was now resting on his gun, its safety snap undone.

"Until America gives back at least its unused public land to the surviving aboriginal people it betrayed, America is a lie," she said. "America's modern day citizens are willing participants in and benefactors of the greatest human tragedy in the history of the modern world, many times worse than Hitler and Nazi Germany during World War II." The restaurant crowd sat breathlessly as Virginia paused, but didn't break her eye contact with the state policeman.

The state policeman wasn't about to let a woman back him down. He'd have to leave town if he lost this argument in front of his cronies and his wife's cousin Richard Redhead. He swallowed the food still left in his mouth, BBQ sauce ran down his chin and dripped on to his pressed shirt.

"That happened a hell of a long time ago. What the hell are we supposed to do about that now?" he demanded.

By now even the cashier had stopped what she was doing and, along with customers, edged within hearing distance of the heated debate. If there was going to be blood shed they wanted to be ring side, and secretly the women rooted from the sidelines rooted for Virginia, the woman.

"Miss, that was a long time ago," Senator Redhead said with a mustered dignity. "Modern America can't give back any land to the Indians."

"Injustice happened and America was founded on stolen lands," Virginia said. "The least the U.S. Government should do is turn over all the unused Government lands back to the American Indians they were stolen from. As it is today, those lands are being mined or treed by multinational companies who are paying nothing or very little for the riches they're removing from the countryside." Dick grew quiet now she was getting a little too close to home.

"Cousin Sam, that sure was some fine eating," Rocco said. It was as if someone had lifted a spell or squirted water on two fighting dogs. The servers and cashier went back to work, people started chewing their food again, everyone began acting as if nothing had happened, as if they had all awakened together from a bad dream, a dream that no one wanted to remember. Father Charles made the Sign of the Cross and kissed the crucifix on the rosary hanging around his neck.

Johnny rose to leave then taking Virginia's hand they turned to toward the cashier. Cousin Sam, however, said proudly that he wouldn't let his cousin Rocco or any of his riding buddies pay for their meals. He also invited them to spend the night next door in his motel as his guests. Virginia and Johnny declined the offer of the over night stay, using the excuse that there was plenty of daylight left and they wanted to push on.

As Johnny and Virginia went out the front door nearly everyone in Sam's diner wished them good luck on their long journey to Taos. Then they were gone before anyone could fully understand what had just taken place in that restaurant.

Tears rolled down Virginia's cheeks as they mounted the bike in the parking lot. Johnny knew now without a doubt that what she said in the restaurant was very close to her heart and secretly he had agreed with everything that she said. He believed she'd done more than open a few eyes in there. At the very least that crowd would begin thinking about their world a little differently from this day on.

Virginia told Johnny she knew of a camping site a few hours out of Jasper. Johnny didn't ask any questions, he just pointed the bike in the northwest direction Virginia had suggested and had headed out of town. They were riding toward the Davy Crocket National Forest near the route the "Discover America One gang" had chosen. Staying on the main highway until they were north of the park, he turned the motorcycle left onto an old overgrown hunting road. Virginia had said that some years ago she'd met friends and camped there. Johnny pulled well down the dirt road completely out of sight of the main highway and turned off the engine. He turned to look at Virginia.

"Virginia, are you sure we aren't on private land?" Johnny asked. Virginia shook her head no. "It looks like no one has driven down this road in years." They only had a few hours of sunlight left and the forest was taking on a beautiful golden late afternoon hue. Virginia reassured Johnny that it would be fine if they drove a little further into the woods and pitched their tent for one night.

"It's probably going to be cool in the forest tonight," she said. "We'll need to gather wood before dark and make a fire." Johnny drove the motorcycle on down the grass-covered one lane dirt road which slowly narrowed into a one lane game trail. Branches from the trees lining the sides had nearly blocked access to the trail, now used only by animals and inhabited by brown jackrabbits that jumped out of their path just ahead of them. After some miles they came to a large clearing with only sparse underbrush and lined with huge ancient virgin trees and a small hill was set in the curve of a creek. Several deer grazed on the edge of the meadow hardly taking notice of Johnny and Virginia. Virginia raised her arm and pointed toward the creek.

"Pull up to that side of the meadow, next to the hill," she said. A rainbow of wild flowers covered the small field. "We'll pitch the tent on the hill top there in case we get rain, it will run away from the tent." Johnny pulled up to the spot Virginia had selected and turned off the engine.

"I hope we don't run out of gas back here, it'd be a long walk back to a civilization," Johnny said. Their bodies tingled from the vibrations of the motorcycle as they slid off the seats and began taking off their helmets. Johnny hung their helmets on the rear view mirrors to keep any rain or dew from gathering in them during the night. "I'm out of shape for this kind of riding. Can you believe we pulled out of Madisonville just this morning?"

"Foley for me," Virginia said. She bent over and began collecting kindling and firewood then taking it up to the top of the hill. "Why don't you pitch the tent near the east end right over there?" she pointed. "The wind is drifting off the creek toward us and that location should keep the smoke away from the tent." Johnny followed Virginia's advice, pitching the tent while watching the evening sky turn bright autumn colors.

By the time Johnny had the tent up and their gear unloaded and inside, Virginia had a pot of coffee ready on a campfire. Johnny walked wearily over to Virginia and sat on the ground next to her rubbing his neck and moaning. Virginia smiled at his collapsed form and handed him a tin cup of steaming hot black coffee along with three aspirins. Johnny smiled back at Virginia as he tossed the aspirins into the back of his throat and washed them down with the hot coffee.

"I hope you're not too hungry?" he said. "I didn't pack much in the way of nourishment." He shrugged his shoulders in a helpless fashion.

"I'm not very hungry," she said. "Not after that fabulous lunch Rocco's cousin fed us today. He was very hospitable and I feel really bad about the way I burst out in there, I don't normally voice my feelings in front of Wasichu."

"What's a Wasichu?" Johnny asked.

"A non native," she said.

"Why not say it," he said. Virginia looked at him not understanding what he meant. "I mean, if you really believe in something, you should speak what you believe."

"You don't realize what it's like do you?" she said. Johnny looked at her now not understanding what she meant. "You look like a Wasichu enough to pass for one. You don't know about the prejudice when people see you are American Indian and even the danger if you show you aren't afraid of their imposed authority. Our people are still expected after all these years to stay on the reservations," she said. "We're not supposed to remind wealthy and middle class Americans that their wealth was and is achieved through the blood of the aboriginal people who were slaughtered like animals for their land.

"We are still here some of us still survive," she said. "Our economy has been deliberately destroyed or taken away from us. Yet Wasichu refuse to let us participate in their society or even exist as a distinct people. The Wasichu rule the economy and run the corporations. We are allowed only minimum wage jobs or jobs of little consequence when we can get one. The Wasichu look at us and tell themselves the Indians are stupid and lazy. They are weird, ugly, primitive and backward. They have no souls. They are only animals. That's why they have nothing, achieve nothing, and are nothing." Johnny sat frozen just like at lunch, amazed and ashamed that he had never given much thought about the conquering of America and the racism, prejudice, and hate inflicted upon the original owners.

"It's true we are a broken people," she said. "The Wasichus have taken away everything we owned, our way of life, the way we supported our families, our homes, even our children are taken away from their families to send them to Wasichu schools. They do this to break our traditions, our culture, our sacred traditions and religion. They have taught our children to be ashamed of their own parents.

"Until recently it was against the law for American Indians to practice their own religion," she said. "Do you hear the absurdity of what I'm saying? Land of the free, home of the brave, founded by Europeans looking for religious freedom. But it has been against Federal law for American Indians to practice their own religion, and they are still hampered in some ways.

"Our sacred ways passed down to us on this continent for at least 12,000 years, long before Jesus Christ walked on this earth in the Middle East," she said. "We are a broken people indeed. However, the shame is on the Wasichu, for genocide, theft, and the economic and religious oppression of Native Americans even today. Our success is against all odds." Virginia paused, finally taking her eyes off Johnny. Johnny gulped down his warm coffee and refilled his cup as Virginia wiped the tears from her face with her shirt sleeve.

"Virginia, I don't know how you can live with so much pain in your heart," he said. "I know almost nothing about my American Indian ancestry. But I do remember the very moment I found out."

"My mother was getting my favorite blanket down from the closet," Johnny said. "I was preschool age and was going to use the blanket to make a tent. The well-worn wool blanket had a Native American pattern on it. My mother leaned over, putting the blanket into my hands lovingly, she whispered to me in a secret conspiratorial tone even though we were alone in the house."

"We have Indian blood in us," she said. "I can still see the fearful look on her face. It's etched into my memory. I could tell even as a child that we weren't supposed to tell anyone, that being a native was to be treated as a second class American. It was better to pretend you weren't if you could."

"The coffee must be cool enough now," she said. "I think I'll have a cup before you drink it all." Johnny laughed at her, sensing her relief at his understanding of her feeling. The world was for the moment a happy place again, the tent was set up, the sleeping bags were rolled out on the pads inside, the crickets were starting to chorus, and the sun was near setting.

"Virginia, I don't think you could have picked a better camping spot," he said. "It's really beautiful here." His eyes scanned the scene and he could feel his energy level picking up from the two cups of hot coffee and the aspirin he swallowed were having their effect. Birds were calling to each other through the trees. Not a single sound of anything man made could be heard as the creek gurgled nearby.

"Listen," Johnny said. "I can hear the creek for the first time. It's pretty loud. Isn't it funny how things can be all around you but unless you slow down long enough you never notice them?" Virginia smiled at him.

"You want to go for a walk?" she asked. "I'll show you something I believe you'll find interesting, if I can still find it." They walked down to the water's edge and followed the sandy bank down stream. Johnny reached down into the sand and picked up an arrowhead three or four inches long, proudly displaying it to Virginia.

"I can't believe I found an Indian arrowhead," Johnny said. "I spent many hours as a kid walking river banks at my grandmother's looking for one." Virginia nodded her head and Johnny slipped the prize into his pocket. Looking ahead he saw a fork in the creek and on an area of higher ground he saw a circle of stones. It appeared to Johnny that a hut had once stood there. About twenty feet in diameter, it was now nearly hidden by sticks and leaves.

"What is it, a burial mound?" Johnny asked.

"No," Virginia answered.

"It looks like the walls of an old stone hut," Johnny said.

"It was a Sweat Lodge," Virginia said. "It's an ancient Sweat Lodge. My husband and I attended a Stone People Ceremony here before we were married. A Medicine Man named White Deer who knew the ancient spiritual ways performed it. It was still a much forbidden ceremony then, against Federal law. Meeting secretly at make-shift areas or forgotten ancient sites was a way to renew ties with our traditions without going to jail. The American Indian Medicine Man is unique," she said.

"Same thing as a Shaman?" Johnny asked.

"Yes, the Shaman has remained untouched by any of the world's other religions. The Turtle Island Shaman alone has remained deeply rooted in nature and the natural elements and is the most pure and powerful form of Shamanism left in the world," she said.

"Where is Turtle Island?" Johnny asked.

"North and South Americas along with the Caribbean are known to many tribes as Turtle Island," she said. "There are Shamans in Europe, Asia, and Africa within the aboriginal peoples there but the Christian, Muslim and Buddhist religions have influenced their present-day beliefs and practices," she continued.

"Shamans are master technicians of altered states of consciousness," she said. "Elusive and secretive now, they were once powerful religious and political forces in the world's people. Shamans, by tradition, suffered social isolation. It wasn't until the Religious Freedom Act of 1978 was passed that the American Indian people were legally allowed to practice parts of their traditional religion again. But after more than a hundred years of persecution by the Federal Government and Wasichu churches the Shaman and the original American people's religious beliefs had gone underground."

"That's hard to believe," Johnny said.

"I know altered states sounds like hocus-pocus to you," she said. "But if you would step back and look at the religion you were raised in, you would find similarities if you wanted to. You know walking on water, burning bushes, bringing people back to life, the blind to see, the parting of the sea, the lame to walk, it's there if you look."

"So the first step to American Indian religious practice is attending a purification ceremony?" he asked.

"Yes," she said. "It's similar to the Christian Baptisms washing away original sin."

"Can you perform one here now?" he asked.

"No," she said. "We should get back to the camp now and check our fire before we get lost in the night," she said. She took the lead back to the campsite, collecting wood along the way to replenish their fire for dinner and to keep it burning into the night.

A damp chill filled the air almost immediately after dark, and an early dew seemed to settle into their clothing as Johnny and Virginia prepared their meager meal of instant soup and crackers. He hadn't packed food for two. They would have to share what he had packed and shop tomorrow for more supplies. After eating dinner they sat by the campfire, neither of them talking much, both staring at the yellow and blue flames dance out of the orange embers. Occasionally sparks leaped up and floated into the night.

"Do you realize, Johnny, that our families have been sitting around campfires just like this since the beginning of time?" Virginia said. Johnny turned to her studying her face for a moment in the glow. She seemed to radiate light from the inside out.

"Virginia, do you think about your husband often?" Johnny asked.

"Yes, nearly all the time," she said.

"I was wondering how I would handle having a helpless spouse?" Johnny said. "I've never had to take care of or worry about anyone but myself."

"In some ways you remind me of him," she said. "He questioned everything he saw and he was a visionary, too."

"I may ask a lot of questions," Johnny said. "But I've never been called a visionary."

"Some of his friends say that's why he developed brain cancer, from evil forces that wanted to stop him from doing good," Virginia said. Johnny wondered about "evil forces" and self-induced trances. He figured all that was possible.

"Do you think he would mind us taking this trip together?" Johnny asked. Johnny wasn't comfortable thinking about sharing a tent with another man's wife, especially a helpless man. Johnny had been raised with a sister and knew how to act as a gentleman, but he wanted to clear the air. The last thing Johnny wanted to do was to fall in love with another man's wife.

"I don't believe he would begrudge me living my life," she said. "I was and am a devoted wife to him. I am still the mother of his child. My mother is taking care of Naichie for me while I'm on this trip. The nursing home is taking care of my husband around the clock, better than I could. I believe I'm entitled to go on with my life. I don't want to sit home and grieve the rest of my life. That would get us nothing. He would want Naichie and me to go on with our lives.

"Johnny, I don't want you to get the wrong idea about me either," she said. "I not looking for a husband, I already have one. That would only cause confusion and grief. But I think it's important that you know I believe you are a good and kind person and I am very glad our paths have crossed."

"Thank you," Johnny told her.

"I'm going to go to sleep now. Good night JT," Virginia said.

"Good night, my friend," he answered and breathed a sigh a relief. She entered her side of the small dome-shaped tent and zipped the flap. He couldn't honestly say he wasn't attracted to Virginia. She was a beautiful and intelligent woman, but respect for her, her invalid husband and her son limited his emotions for her.

Within minutes he could hear Virginia's breathing slow and lengthen as sleep over took her. That was Johnny's cue to make sure the fire was all right before he called it a night himself. Slowly he unzipped the flap on his side of the tent and crawled inside out of the cool night air. He lay in the tent and watched the flame less coals burn bright red emitting a slow curl of smoke nearly straight up into the black night sky. A forest orchestra of ten thousand insect and animal sounds just outside the glow of the fire.

He thought about how humankind had never embraced the full potential of spirituality in which many claimed to believe. If a person could stand away from their particular cultural mirage they would see the world in all its brutish savagery and natural beauty. Spiritually enlightened persons would be moved to realize truth, the meaning of love, and so the value of the natural environment as well as it's human inhabitants.

He wondered if God had been gently calling humans back to the Garden of Eden ever since they had left. In a funny sort of way, it made sense to Johnny. When God created humankind in the Garden of Eden, he didn't give man permission to chop down all the trees or kill all the animals, that would have obviously been a stupid thing to do because they would have perished shortly thereafter. Still it seemed obvious to Johnny in the firelight that humankind was still walking further away from the Garden and still didn't get it. Was there a way to turn humankind around to start him walking back in the right direction, Johnny wondered! Salvation or extinction-two opposites-he thought.

Remembering his own discovery today in the sand at the creek, Johnny pulled the arrowhead out of his pocket and inspected it by the glowing light of the coals. The soft light gave a pinkish tint to the marble white stone, which had been carefully shaped into a classic spear or arrow point. Johnny had admired relics for years in collections and various antique shops, but knowing that they had been dug from a human graves prevented him from ever purchasing any of the beautiful pieces. To do so would have been the equivalent of being a grave robber or a profiteer of it. Having found this one today naturally exposed on the creek was a wonderful surprise or gift, he pondered it's story.

Johnny grabbed the bag he used for storing the tent and pulled out the leather lace he kept for emergency repairs. Taking off a three-foot-long piece of raw hide he moistened it from the canteen and stretched it around the narrow square end of the arrowhead the end normally attached to the shaft. As the leather dried it would shrink and become permanently attached to the man-shaped stone. He took the remaining two and one half feet and made a big Loop to serve as a chain around his neck. Checking his craftsmanship, he slipped the arrowhead necklace over his head and around his neck hiding it all under his shirt.

He slipped into his sleeping bag and fell asleep watching the campfire's occasional flames shadow dance on the roof of the tent.

Early the next morning with the sun barely beginning to show the promise of a new day, Virginia unintentionally woke Johnny while rekindling the fire. Johnny gave her a weak salutation.

"I'm going to make some coffee, would you like a cup?" she asked.

"I'd love a cup," he said. "I slept straight through the night, how about you?"

"I slept very well, thank you," she relied. "But I dreamed all night about our trip." Johnny sat up slowly, rubbing the sleep from his eyes, trying to focus on Virginia as she moved about the fire with grace and confidence, Johnny never tired of watching her move.

"What about the trip?" he asked. The second she had said the word "dream," Johnny had a flashback of a dream he was having just before she woke him.

"I dreamed that we arrived at our final destination and that Michael, my husband, was riding with us," she said. Johnny pulled on his blue jeans and climbed out of the sleeping bag.

"What was our destination?" he asked. Virginia turned and gave Johnny a goofy smile through the netting.

"I don't know. I mean, I knew in my dream, but I don't know now," she said.

They broke camp, rolled the tent and sleeping bags up and attached it all back on the FXR. It was getting much easier to attach the gear to the bike now. Everything seemed to know its own place.

"Virginia, did we spend the night on an Indian mound?" Johnny asked and Virginia gave Johnny a puzzled look. "This mound of dirt is the only hill around here," he said.

"Yes, it is Johnny," she said. "Did you have any dreams last night?"

"Yeah," he said. "I dreamed I won 82 million dollars in a lottery."

"Wow, Johnny, I guess your dream was in color, too, huh?" Virginia teased. Johnny blushed and tried to change the subject.

"I don't remember," he said. "We'll need to get gasoline for the bike pretty quickly once we get back out to civilization. I can't wait to get in a shower. There's this place called the Big Texan over in Amarillo. They've got live country music and a menu with rattlesnake on it."

"Rattlesnake! Johnny, give me a break, I mean a steak," she said. Johnny laughed as she climbed on the back of the Harley. He fired it up and idled back toward the highway, dodging bushes and tree limbs he hadn't notice on the drive into camp the evening before. He even scared up a spotted fawn that had bedded down by the side of the trail during the night.

"I didn't say I'd eat it," he said. "I just said they have it on the menu. Anyway, I figure that's where we'll find Pim and Rocco tonight." Johnny and Virginia came out on the blacktop highway just as the sun made its way completely above the horizon of bright green tree tops. The forest on both sides of the road formed a wall, almost a tunnel of thick leaves waving back and forth in the morning breeze.

Johnny slipped the bike in neutral and zipped up his jacket all the way to the neck. Her face was completely covered by the helmet and face shield.

"Virginia, you didn't buy that biker coat just for this trip did you?" he asked

"Nope, I've had it for a long time," she said. He wanted to ask the history of the coat but didn't. When he let out on the clutch and cracked the throttle, the bike responded eagerly and roared into the morning. The sky was a clear blue, the Harley was purring, and today the world was a happy place, Johnny thought.

"Hey, Virginia," Johnny said. "Thanks for coming along. The trip wouldn't have been the same without you."

"What?" she yelled back over the noise. Johnny pushed the gearshift lever into fifth gear and accelerated the bike into a long uphill turn. He felt the arrowhead necklace pressed against his chest.

"Nothing, I'll tell you later," he said.

BIG TEXAN

"Hello Karen, this is Lee. I'm worried about Johnny, I've been trying to reach him for days. He doesn't return my telephone pages," Lee said. "The marina tells me he asked them to keep a close watch on his boat for a few weeks. Have you heard anything?"

"There is no telling with that guy," she said. "He could be off half way around the world, I just wish he'd settle down and raise a family, he would make a great father."

"Yeah," Lee said. "But I'm not so sure about the husband part. Did he mention anything to you about getting some money?"

"No," she said. "Well, yes, he said something about a lump sum he might get. What do you know that you're not telling me?"

"Nothing really, he's probably been working a lot over time, that's all." He realized Karen had no idea Johnny was a multimillionaire.

"No telling where he's at," Lee said. "But if you get any news or hear from him, let me know." Lee folded up his cell telephone and stopped his golf cart at the Mallard Cove golf course ninth hole. This was his worst hole although it was simple enough. Somehow, the golf trolls always screwed with him on this hole.

Not today, though Lee told himself, he would not let them. He was two under par on the ninth hole and if his luck held out, he'd beat the local golf pro out of $150 before lunch. He grabbed his driver and walked up to the pro.

"You want to make a side bet, of say fifty bucks?" Lee asked.

The wind was dry and high on the western plains that afternoon. So high, in fact, that Johnny and Virginia had to lean sharply into the wind to keep the motorcycle on the road. Riding almost sideways down the highway at 70 miles per hour wasn't the worst part, though. The wind wasn't consistent, and when it would let up, as it occasionally did, the bike would veer and Johnny had to rapidly straighten out or run off the highway. Straightening out wasn't that hard to do rapidly, unless he was also dodging road-kill, a pothole, or even worse, a moving ball of tumbleweed. Just as its name suggests, tumbleweed would appear out of nowhere rolling across the road with no warning. Johnny had heard stories about tumbleweeds colliding with motorcycles, and it could be deadly.

The last couple of hours driving toward Amarillo were so grueling he wondered if they would make it all the way. The evening sky had darkened and become overcast making the riding monotonous. With little to look at but the perpetual dusk and the West Texas prairie. They hadn't passed any decent places to spend the night or they surely would have given up on making it to the Big Texan Motel and Restaurant. The only thing that had kept Johnny going on was the hope that Pim and Rocco would show up at the Big Texan like they had planned back before the trip began.

From the very beginning of planning the trip, they had agreed to take small roads through little towns. Eventually the journey had become nicknamed the "Discover America One." I was called that because they would be cruising through territory that none of them had ever seen before. Except for an occasional national food or retail chain, most of the small towns were dotted with family-owned, mom-and-pop stores and cafes, tiny wood framed houses with ordinary people trying to make ends meet. Farms and ranches with their cowboys and Indians and Spanish added to the scene.

Amarillo was really a small town compared to Houston, Dallas, or El Paso, but after crossing those long, lonesome prairies, he and Virginia felt as if they had pulled into Las Vegas, Nevada. At first, there had been feed lots, then truck stops, finally a few motels, and by the time they reached the Big Texan, the highway was crowded with city traffic and eighteen wheelers loaded with cattle or freight.

The signs advertising the Big Texan's restaurant and motel began miles before Amarillo, before much of anything but West Texas, prairie, the kind of advertisements older travelers would remember as children riding with their parents on vacations after World War II or migrating during the Great Depression. The kind of advertisements travelers had probably witnessed since the beginnings of communications, before advertising companies, before national and international corporations, and mass production. The Big Texan didn't have any circus sideshows, but it did have live music, clean motel rooms, hot showers, good food, live music some nights, and on Tuesday nights a live country revue, any of which was exciting after two days on the road.

Johnny and Virginia pulled into the parking lot, coasting to a slow stop in front of the motel office. Johnny was not sure if his legs had enough strength left to hold up the bike. So, as insurance, he put down the kickstand before Virginia swung her leg off to dismount. Johnny leaned the bike over on the kickstand before he climbed off and stretched his cramped muscles, twisting and cracking his back, neck, and joints slowly he brought his body completely to an erect posture. He stood there waiting for feeling to come back to his legs, eventually he hoped to walk toward the motel office door. Virginia was smiling at his movements but felt just as road weary.

"Johnny, if you don't mind, I think I'll wait out here for you," she said. She was standing out by the bike and resting against the seat. The bike's engine was ticking like a wind up clock as it cooled down in the late evening air.

The sun was just barely visible behind the giant neon Big Texan sign. Shaped liked a cowboy it stood sixty feet tall. Restaurant patrons in the parking lot going to or from their cars craned their necks to see the two wind-swept riders. Johnny and Virginia were too road weary to worry about their new audience and paid them no attention. Johnny had noticed before that Harley Davidsons made people stare. He'd guessed some people were looking to see if a motorcycle gang member had arrived but most of the time he figured they were bikers or want-to-be bikers imagining what life would be like on the road.

The motel office was large and well furnished. The desk clerk smiled politely and didn't seem to notice Johnny's appearance. She quickly found his reservation, confirmed his personal credit card information then handed him the room keys. Johnny dropped them into his helmet like it was a purse.

"We have a complimentary breakfast," she said. "Here in the lobby starting at 6:00 A.M." Johnny thanked her making a mental note to take advantage of the breakfast.

Johnny had reserved a ground floor room, so that he could park the bike inside the room at night while he slept. Although he didn't mention that to the receptionist she probably had seen it done many times before. Motorcycles were not like cars. If a car was gone in the morning there was a problem sure, but if a motorcycle was gone in the morning, most motorcycle enthusiasts would have felt as though they had lost a member of the family. Johnny carefully pushed the bike completely into the safety of the motel room.

Virginia claimed rights to the first shower, again, Johnny flipped through the channels on the TV wondering if Rocco and Pim would show up. Just seconds later he heard the sound of someone driving a motorcycle from the parking lot into the room next door. Johnny set down the remote control and stepped out his motel room door in his socks just in time to see Rocco ride his bike over the yellow parking lot curb nearly popping a wheely and attacking the threshold with the same look of determination as he disappeared into the echoing motel room.

Looking around the parking lot to see who might have noticed the display of macho stupidity, Johnny walked over to Rocco's door and looked cautiously in. Rocco was sitting on the edge of the bed in the unlighted room staring into space with his helmet in his lap. The motorcycle's engine ticked as it cooled and the room smelled of hot exhaust.

"Hey, Rocco," Johnny said. "You're not afraid of pissing off the management riding your motorcycle in the motel room? I usually just push mine in quiet as I can."

"I don't give a flying @#$!" Rocco exploded.

"What's your problem?" Johnny questioned.

"Pim rode off and left me," Rocco said.

"Where did he leave you?" Johnny asked.

"Early this morning-you know how sometimes we ride out in front when we get bored," Rocco said. "Maybe exceed the speed limit for a little while. You know eventually the front rider is supposed to stop or slow down enough so his friends can catch up with him." Rocco stopped talking, rose, and started removing his bags from the bike.

"Yeah, and so then what," Johnny said. Rocco looked over at Johnny, trying to get his temper under control. His face had three days of beard growth and was covered with whelps and smashed bugs from the road trip. Rocco was a purist and didn't believe in windshields on his bike, at least on this first road trip.

"Well, Pim pulled out shortly after we left Cousin Sam's in Jasper and I haven't seen him since," Rocco said. Johnny stood there watching Rocco throw his gear around the room. Considering the circumstantial evidence there was one obvious chink in the story that Rocco had related.

"Well, if Pim is ahead of you then how did you beat him here?" Johnny said. "He should have shown up here like we planned last week." Rocco pondered the mystery, sitting down on the bed again. Pulling off his boots he turned to Johnny with a concerned look on his face.

"You haven't seen or heard from him either?" Rocco asked. Johnny shook his head no and then as though on cue, the two of their heads turned to look out the door when they heard the unmistakable sound of a Harley Davidson pulling up to the motel office. They stuck their heads out of the door, Rocco struggling to get his boots back on. Pim sat on his bike unbuckling his helmet in the quickly fading daylight. Johnny laughed a loud laugh of relief.

"Rocco, why don't you and Pim meet Virginia and me in the dining room?" Johnny said. Rocco looked at his watch, then glanced over at Pim.

"Ok, we'll meet you guys at nine," he said.

Johnny walked back to his room and let himself in with his room key. Virginia was already camping out on her bed with the TV on and the remote in her hand. Her hair was wrapped in a white motel towel and she looked completely relaxed.

"I hope you're hungry?" he said to her. "The receptionist told me they're having some kind of talent competition tonight in the restaurant." Virginia turned her attention away from the television and looked at Johnny.

"Don't worry about me," she said. "Those chili dogs we had at the Dairy Queen seven hours ago have faded into the sunset. Or however they say it out here in cowboy land." Johnny laughed out loud. It didn't take much to make him laugh most of the time. Right now, he was especially happy to be off the road with the prospect of good company and a hot meal. The world was looking good.

"What kind of competition are they having?" she said. "A chili cook off?" Johnny laughed again. He looked at Virginia, sitting now on the end of her bed. Her face was red from the dry prairie winds and sun and she had on no make up. She was wearing a pair of ragged cut off blue jean shorts and a sweatshirt, he hadn't known her to be a comedian, he thought. He guessed she had been emotionally down about personal things yesterday when she ambushed that table of Jasper locals trying to have lunch. Johnny looked at her, trying to keep a straight face.

"No, Jay Leno," he said. "I don't think it's a food competition at all. Although that's a good guess considering it's taking place in a restaurant."

"The receptionist said it was something of a local music talent contest," he said. "However, when they say local around here, I imagine their talking about a 200-mile radius."

"Music, that's interesting," she said. "Let me take another wild guess, it probably won't be rap music." Virginia herself burst out laughing this time.

"You know that's the first time I've ever seen you heehaw, no pun intended," he smiled. "We must be exhausted. Listen to us, we sound like a couple of grammar school kids having a sleep over. I'm going to take a shower. Rocco and Pim are going to meet us in less than an hour in the restaurant lobby, if you like country music."

"I love country music, if the food is good," she said.

Still laughing, Johnny got a change of clothes out of his bag, and a little zip-lock bag of laundry detergent. He always kept detergent handy when he traveled to hand wash his dirty clothes nights when he was in a hotel. Hotels, generally speaking, couldn't get laundry back before an early check-out time and certainly not by daylight.

"Hey, slow poke, they're walking over to the restaurant now," Virginia yelled through the bathroom door. Johnny came out of the bathroom and hung his wet clothes on the room air conditioner vent. Grabbing a pair of clean dry socks from his bag, he sat on the end of his bed to put his boots back on. Virginia stood and waited by the door, watching TV.

"I can't imagine why I'm so hungry," she said laughing. "But if I don't eat soon, I'm going to be sick." Johnny walked over to her and put his hand on her forehead.

"We must have burned 6000 calories hanging onto that bike in the wind today," he said. "It's no wonder you're hungry." He ushered her though the door and closed it behind them.

As they walked across the parking lot, heading for the steps at the front door of the Big Texan, they could see Rocco and Pim sitting on a bench watching the parking lot as females walked by. Virginia and Johnny climbed the stairs to the bench by the entrance where Rocco and Pim sat.

"Check out this menu," Pim said. "They got rattlesnake, buffalo burgers, frog legs, and Texas jack rabbit."

"Yeah, well, I ain't eating none of that stuff," Rocco said. "I can tell you right now I'm going to get me one of those big four and one-half pound steaks. The signs along the highway said you get it free if you eat it all." Rocco looked at Virginia.

"I guess you're going to get one of those fancy dishes, huh, pretty girl," Rocco teased. Virginia leaned over toward Rocco, looked deep in his eyes and gave him a big grin, then snatched the menu from his hands before he knew what she was up to.

"If you don't mind I'll choose my own dinner," she said. "Right now I'm so hungry I could eat a couple of those rattlesnakes," she teased back.

The lobby was full of people waiting to be seated. They milled around the gift shop looking at the Big Texan's display of the odd and unusual. Almost everything displayed had a Western accent. After a ten-minute wait, the hostess found them a non-smoking table on the far side of the huge room. There was a stage set up in the middle and the master of ceremonies was talking into a microphone standing center stage.

Singing contestants from various categories with their friends and families were standing and seated all over the room. A curly haired, red-headed, freckled teenage girl wearing a red plaid square dance outfit and a white pressed short-sleeve blouse was singing her heart out on the "Yellow Rose of Texas."

A waitress came to their table and passed out the big laminated menus, waiting to take the before-dinner drink orders.

"I'll have a draft," Rocco told the waitress. Virginia turned in her seat.

"Have what you like. Dinner is on me," Virginia announced. They all told her to forget about that, this was a Dutch treat dinner. Virginia surrendered her offer. She only wanted to be forgiven for the scene she caused at Sam's Diner in Jasper, but the guys acted like they had already forgotten about it.

They ordered appetizers of rattlesnake and Texas jack rabbit. Both Pim and Rocco went for the giant steaks, and Virginia and Johnny decided to split a seafood platter.

"Probably a mistake," she said, as soon as the waitress left.

"What do you mean?" Johnny asked, thinking the same thing.

"You know," she said. "Ordering seafood out here in the middle of cattle country." They both shrugged their shoulders.

"I'm going to try out the soup at the salad bar," Virginia announced. Pim and Rocco stood and followed her over like milk cows with full udders following the dairy farmer.

"Hey, guys, don't you think if you're fixing to enter an eating contest it might wise to skip the soups and appetizers?" Virginia asked. Rocco and Pim looked at each other and without saying a word walked back to the table staring at the floor. Johnny sat, watching people, trying to figure out who were the locals and who were the tourists.

As everyone was seated back at the table, an American Indian looking woman with straight black hair took the stage. He could hear the people at the table behind them saying that she was the Indian woman Sacheen Little Feather, the one who had spoken about the cruelty of the United States Government to the American Indians. That was at the 1972 Academy Awards "The Godfather" award which Marlon Brando declined to accept in protest.

Johnny was surprised people still remembered about that. The world hadn't been shocked when Brando's name was announced for the Oscar. However, they were very shocked when an American Indian looking woman dressed in traditional clothes walked on stage. At the microphone, she denounced the United States genocide of its Native American population. But that had been decades ago.

Johnny watched her now on the Big Texan's stage expecting her to speak about genocide, but, instead she sang a soulful native ballad in English and was rewarded with a lot of applause.

When she went to a small table against the wall to sit alone Virginia stood and excused herself to jon her. Soon the food was served and Virginia noticed that Rocco, Pim, and Johnny were letting their food get cold waiting for her so she returned to her traveling companions.

Johnny and Virginia loved their food, even the rattlesnake appetizers. Rocco and Pim moved to a special table and after a mighty struggle had eaten all of their steaks. They started laughing believing they had beaten the restaurant and won their steaks with five minutes left on their one-hour time limit. The waitress came to check on them and politely announced.

"I'm sorry, when the advertisement say's all, it means all, including the gristle, the salad and the baked potato," The waitress said.

"Can't do it," Pim said immediately, pushing away from the table. He wiped his face and hands looking embarrassed and disgusted. "I can't eat a mound of gristle, not if I want to get any sleep tonight, not even counting the potato and salad, I'm just not that cheap."

"I believe I can do it," Rocco said. "In fact, the fat is my favorite part, I was just trying to be healthy. But hell for the fifty-dollar price of a giant steak, watch this," Rocco started shoveling gristle with a skill that proved years of practice. None of them could stand to watch Rocco gorge himself. In less than the allotted five minutes remaining, he finished everything. Grease dripped down his chin and he belched uncontrollably as he smiled, the sight was beyond repulsive.

Johnny rose with Virginia and announced they would see them in the morning. Pim refused to let go of the check, so after thanking him Virginia and Johnny walked back through the parking lot to their room.

"Remind me to check the motorcycle's oil in the morning before we take off," he said.

"No problem," she replied preoccupied with thoughts of home. Virginia made a very proficient first mate and It made Johnny feel warm inside to know that someone as good as Virginia enjoyed being with him.

"What did the American Indian singer have to say?" Johnny said. Virginia unlocked the door with her key motioning Johnny to go first. Johnny did as she asked and Virginia followed.

"We didn't have a lot of time to talk, but she said she would try to meet us at the sweat lodge in Taos," she said. "You sleep with the television on or off?" she asked Johnny. He closed the door behind them.

"I set the sleep timer to thirty minutes," he said. "I'm usually asleep by then. Did my snoring bother you in the tent last night?"

"No, I thought it was the ghost of the Indian mound," she said with a giggle. "Good night."

"Good night," he said. "Don't forget to say your prayers." Virginia smiled and Johnny rolled over on his side and closed his eyes.

"I say prayers all during the day," she said. "Good night."

Johnny began dreaming about the end of the world. He was a small boy again, standing alone in a dark forest at night. Trees were groaning, creaking and crashing down all around in a hurricane-like storm, but he wasn't afraid for himself. A recurring dream as a child when his parents had still been alive he would jump in their bed to protect them.

Somewhere in the distance, a telephone was ringing.

"Hello," he said. His lips were barely able to speak.

"Hello, how are y'all feeling over there?" Pim said.

"Great," Johnny said. "I guess I slept straight through."

"Me too," whispered Virginia.

"What time is it?" Johnny said.

"It's about five o'clock and the time is a wasting," Pim said.

"Are you all ready to go?" Johnny said. He was trying to get a grasp of what Pim wanted. Pim chuckled through Johnny's earpiece.

"I am, but Rocco's just getting out of bed," Pim said. "Are we riding together today?" Johnny looked over at Virginia, who now appeared to be sleeping again.

"Yeah, sure, I mean, if y'all want to," he said. He sat up in the bed and flipped on the lamp switch by his head. His watch said three after five in the morning.

The four of them agreed to skip a formal sit down breakfast and to grab some donuts and coffee from the motel office. Rocco was still sick from the steak dinner the night before and was not interested in bacon and eggs.

Virginia and Johnny got dressed and pushed the FXR back through the motel room door and out into the parking lot. Johnny asked Virginia to hold the bike straight up while he checked the oil level. He didn't trust the dipstick when the bike was leaning on the kickstand, although it probably didn't matter that much.

There wasn't an unused spot on the bike when they had finished loading their gear. Johnny threw his right leg over the FXR and lifted it off the kickstand. Virginia knew the routine and without a spoken word she followed Johnny's lead and climbed aboard the back of the bike. Johnny went through the ritual of turning the key, pulling the choke, flipping the throttle once, and then firing it up. They idled over to the office without their helmets on. No matter how many times Johnny started the Harley, it always got his heart pumping.

Johnny got a weather report from the receptionist, windy and cool, the same as yesterday and the day before. He gave her back the keys to the room and checked out. Pim and he stuffed two donuts each, in their mouths and headed outside with coffee and donuts for Rocco and Virginia. Virginia collected everyone's trash and deposited it in the wastebasket just inside the office door, then climbed back aboard the FXR behind Johnny.

The three bikes headed to the gas station down the service road from the Big Texan. Rocco was last to pull into the service station. Having spent considerable time in the bathroom that night, he was still feeling queasy from dinner. Virginia and Johnny refueled their bike, paid for their gas, and pulled away from the pumps. In their excitement to resume the journey, they felled to notice Rocco hadn't yet gotten off his bike to fuel up. Stopping by the service road at the edge of the gas station parking lot Johnny turned around and looked over Virginia's shoulder to see how far behind Pim and Rocco were, before pulling out on the road.

A grand spectacle had been set in motion. Rocco had just dismounted and put down the kickstand with the engine still running. Reaching up to unbuckle his helmet, he let go of the clutch lever with his left hand the bike lurched off the kickstand and riderless headed across the parking lot at an idle. Rocco had failed to shift the bike into neutral and what followed paralleled the act of a circus trainer with a trick pony. He held onto the left handle bar with his right hand jogging along to keep the bike from taking a nosedive onto the concrete. This acrobatic feat was being accomplished while running in irregular loops avoiding the gas pumps and the cashier's office window. Behind the window the cashier sat, open jawed and motionless.

Rocco was unable to keep the bike balanced upright and pull in the clutch at the same time. Locked in a circle, holding up his motorcycle and flapping his left arm in the air trying to attract help, he looked ridiculous.

Unfolding in slow motion Pim threw his bike in neutral and leaned it on the kickstand and leaped off. He raced toward Rocco, who was still leading the Wide Glide around in circles. Pim posed waiting for Rocco to pass by and then ran along on the opposite side of the bike. Reaching over the handlebars, Pim grabbed the clutch and the brake, stopping the bike and ending the too-odd-to-be-real scene.

"You wouldn't believe what just happened," Johnny said. He turned to Virginia where she sat looking at the red light and wondering why they hadn't pulled out into the road yet. Virginia's eye connected with Johnny's.

"What just happened?" Virginia asked and turned to look at Rocco and Pim. She saw Rocco preparing to fill his gas tank and Pim fastening his helmet. Virginia looked at Johnny with a puzzled look on her face.

"What," she said. Johnny shook his head.

"Remind me to tell you tonight," he said smiling in disbelief. Johnny felt partly responsible for Rocco's near crash in the service station so he turned his bike around and pulled back up to the pumps next to Rocco.

"Rocco, that was a close call. You all right, you want a cold drink?" he asked.

"No, I'm all right," Rocco said. He looked around embarrassed, hoping no one else had seen what hapened. The cashier was smiling brightly at Rocco now through the plate glass window. Rocco went in, to pay for his gas. As he climbed back on his bike, the cashier waved at them. All three bikes pulled out of the parking lot and up onto the highway at the same time. Accelerating and shifting through the gears, the Harley Davidson noise echoed off the buildings nearby. People within earshot turned to watch the riders heading out.

Morning traffic was roaring with the sound of eighteen wheeler tires humming on the concrete, but the eager riders hardly took notice. The wind was just as strong as the day before, but the sky had turned crystal blue. The further they rode out of Amarillo, the thinner the traffic became. Pressing the speed limit, they made good time, stopping only for gas or to look at the map. It was afternoon when they pulled off Highway 54 at Tucumcari, New Mexico.

While refueling on the edge of town, a couple of local bikers rode by wearing no helmets, causing the Discover America Gang to look at them with envy.

"I don't think they have helmet laws here," Johnny said, and the four of them looked at each other smiling.

"I'm taking mine off," Pim said. He got off his bike and attached his helmet to the sissy bar on his FXR. Everyone else followed suit.

Tucumcari was a small western town where no sky scrappers existed and only a few commercial buildings off the main drag. Rocco took out the map and announced that they should take the scenic route.

There was no protest from the group and within a few minutes, they were out on a red desert highway. The landscape was flat, wide and slow to change with long stark, eroded hills that went on for miles in the distance. The turf became more and more barren and the soil redder, the color of southwest clay pottery. The scene was red desert to the horizon on both sides of the road.

Later, long past the point where they needed a rest, the Discover America One gang spotted an old mission not far off the highway they pulled off down a narrow small dirt road that led to a tiny white adobe church several miles off the main road.

There appeared to be ruins of ancient American Indian dwellings not far from the church. A large complex of crumbling stone and mud walls stood out starkly in the distance. From the highway all they had seen was the small old church and that had been enough to distract them from their journey. Since entering the desert that day they had begun to ride slower, even stopping occasionally to look at odd scenes, flowers, the cactus, rock formations.

"Looks like some kind of ancient neighborhood," Pim said. He stopped his bike and looked past where the church stood and pointed his finger. "I believe it was fairly common for the early Christian Churches to build on top of the ancient holy sites of native people," he said. "I read in National Geographic that down in Mexico the Conquistadors would often knock down the native sites of worship and build on top of them."

"This church looks pretty old," Rocco said. "It could be well over a hundred years old." They all got off their bikes and started walking among the ruins.

"Don't touch or pick up anything, it's sacred," Virginia said. Everyone looked at her.

"Why?" Johnny asked? "I mean, how do you know?" Virginia stared blankly at Johnny, wondering if she should say more.

"It's in alignment with the sunrise," said Virginia. "The ancients were great astrologers. The seasons were central themes in their lives. They believed that life was a circle, like the four seasons. They kept up with the solstice and the equinox to regulate the planting and the harvesting of their crops and the hunting and fishing cycles."

SACRED AND HOLY

White Deer, a Medicine Man of the nearly extinct Huron tribe, was literally a man without a country. The Europeans had pursued his people relentlessly.

A fiercely independent and nomadic people who traveled a thousand miles or more between their summer and winter lands. Only a few had managed to survive the European invasions and the diseases that came with them. Some of his people had intermarried with the French during the French and Indian wars, surviving physically, they surrendered their ancient culture. Many Hurons had aligned themselves with the French against the English as the battle for dominance was fought for the New World. The French had made efforts to live among the Indians, learning their customs, languages and often intermarrying, whereas the English generally looked down upon races other than themselves, including the Indians and the French.

Eventually the English gained control of the Huron ancestral lands and did not forget the Hurons' allegiance to the French, the Huron people were hunted to near extinction. A few escaped, joining other tribes, or survived by hiding in Canada. Without their native hunting and fishing lands they were a destroyed culture.

White Deer's parents descended from those peoples who had hidden in the wilderness after the wars. and eventually moved to the Canadian wilderness to avoid the Europeans as much as possible. By the time White Deer reached the age of twelve, the elders of his tribe had seen his interest in the spiritual ways of medicine men, a calling within the native people that was as honorable as a calling to become a preacher or priest among the Europeans. Therefore, from the age of twelve he trained with the only remaining tribal Medicine Man.

Long ago White Deer had decided to avoid the European life style, not because he disliked the Europeans as a whole, but because much of what he felt from his native beliefs was contrary to their material culture. He found that the Christian religious beliefs held many things in common with his people's spiritual beliefs, but, he could not see that the Anglo-men understood the teachings of their own Christian religions.

Not to respect Grandmother Earth was incomprehensible to White Deer. After all, Grandmother Earth and Grandfather Knowledge were the creators and providers for people of all races. To disrespect them, to harm the earth, was to disrespect Grandmother and Grandfather, their creators and their One God.

Native people didn't believe in owning land. They believed they were children of the land born from the earth. Just like the Christian religion tells her believers God created man from dust. Dust to dust. Ashes to ashes. He'd read it with his own eyes from the King James Christian Bible.

White Deer had dedicated his life to the preservation and practice of his people's Medicine Man ways. To live in poverty was a very small sacrifice. His personal needs were small. The biggest problem White Deer found with his spiritual walk in life was that nearly all people he came in contact with valued a person in accordance to their monetary prowess. This was the opposite of what The Great Spirit had shown White Deer's people.

Very little time was left for the people of the world to continue their abuse of the earth. A friend of White Deer's had seen a warning in a vision. Much water would come over the earth but it would be undrinkable.

This and other things Mother Earth and Father Knowledge had said caused White Deer to believe that nuclear energy and its by-products had become a major modern day destructive force.

The Catholic's Blessed Virgin Mary had come as a vision to children in Bosnia and in Mexico, warning the children of great destruction and human suffering if the people of the world did not turn back to God. Not enough people seemed to be listening or really to believe anymore White Deer thought.

A woman friend of White Deer's had called and told him that there was a person who wished to be instructed on the seven levels of the spirit world. White Deer had begun to pray and meditate so that he might know what to say to this seeker coming to see him. White Deer had made a vow not to walk away from anyone truly seeking spiritual understanding.

Virginia had suggested a Sweat Lodge ceremony, the first of the spiritual steps toward understanding, this would be a way for them to meet. White Deer asked Virginia to bring her friend whenever possible. He lived near the Pueblo in Taos, it was not his tribe, but he was accepted there.

Johnny was the first to walk out to the far side of the ruins, ahead of Rocco and Pim. What he found at the edge mystified him.

"Hey, Virginia, is this an altar of some kind?" he asked. Virginia walked over and looked at the collection of stones. There were little sacks tied in bundles placed on a flat rock near bits of recently burned cedar and traces of sage.

"What are you people doing here?" an angry voice yelled only a few feet behind the four of them. They all turned around at once, preparing a posture to defend themselves. They presumed that they had found the owner of the altar.

"We're just sightseeing," Pim said. "I mean we are not going to touch anything, we know better than that." A red-faced preacher stood in front of them, glaring.

"Good gracious, you scared the hell out of us," Rocco said. The preacher stood staring, trying to figure out if he was in danger or not.

"You a Baptist preacher," Rocco asked.

"Yes, Baptist," he said and offered nothing else.

"So am I," Rocco said. "I mean, I'm not a preacher but I go to a Baptist Church."

"What are you people doing out here?" the preacher said.

"Joy riding," Pim said.

"You guys out on a joy ride in this barren country?" the preacher said. He finally lowered his voice and seemed to visibly relax.

"Yeah, we're just on a romp to Taos that's all," Pim said.

"We saw your quaint church here and came out to admire it," Rocco acknowledged. "We didn't know about these ruins, we noticed them after we got here. We weren't going to touch anything, really."

"Yeah, I'm sorry about screaming at you guys," the preacher said. "But I get so tired of these local people coming over here to practice their pagan religion. I usually see them in my church here on Sundays," the preacher said, "but then they're always sneaking over here for secret ceremonies. I've warned them how Jesus doesn't want his children worshiping false gods, but that doesn't seem to bother them."

"Oh," said Virginia.

"Let me start over," he said. "My name is Jimmy James, the church sent me down here two years ago. I'd felt I was doing very little good at my old congregation back up in Michigan so I asked for a transfer five years ago. I would have never asked for a move had I known what I was coming to."

"So you grew up around Detroit?" Rocco asked.

"No, I grew up in Alaska," Preacher James said. "My father moved our family up there back in the sixties to help build the Alaskan pipeline. I knew some westernized Eskimos growing up, and I figured it wouldn't be bad out West. But these American Indians out here are a different breed all together."

"I spent a few years in Alaska myself," Pim said. "You're right about a different people. I've read that they don't even share the same genetics." The preacher nodded his head.

"I try and teach these folks Christianity," The preacher said. "But they hold onto their old ways like their lives depend on it. I'll have to admit though I don't have an inkling about what their beliefs are. They're always so damned secretive about their goings on."

"Maybe if you didn't yell at them when they come to pray out here, they would be more open," Virginia scowled. "Have you ever tried to find any similarities between the two religions?"

"No, and I don't believe anything that's not Christianity is a real religion," Preacher James said. "It's just a superstition or worse, devil worship, far as I can tell or care to know."

"Devil worship?" Johnny questioned. "I guess I can see where you're coming from on that. But you know they believe in one God just like you and me."

"Yeah, one God," the preacher said. "But they also look for guidance from spirits, too—water, fire, wind or rock spirits, stuff like that. That's the work of the devil if you ask me."

"Well, you know Catholics pray to saints and the Virgin Mary," Johnny said.

"Yeah, well the Catholics picked that stuff up over the centuries trying to make their religion fit all the different pagan religions they assimilated within Europe," the preacher said.

"Don't Baptists believe in the Holy Spirit?" Virginia asked. The preacher looked at Virginia then changed the subject.

"I try to make it as simple as possible for them," The preacher said. "But they keep sneaking off to worship their spirits."

"How do you make it simple?" Virginia asked.

"Well for instance, just this past Sunday," the preacher said. "Church was about seeking God, I showed them three cups. One was empty, one was full of ping pong balls, and one was half full of dried corn kernels. I told them that the corn represented the things we need to survive like food, water and money, and the ping pong balls represented God. I told them if you spend all your time trying to get those things like food, water, and money-I poured the corn into the empty cup-there won't be enough room for God in your life. Then I tried to stuff the ping pong balls in the cup with the corn and they wouldn't all fit."

"I told them," The Preacher said "that if they put God first in their life and I put all the ping pong balls into the empty cup. Then all the rest of things they needed would fall into place. Then I took the corn and poured it slowly around the edges working it in until all the corn and the ping-pong balls fit in one cup. Well, those Indians appeared to really approve of that. I think some of them even applauded."

"But the very next day," The preacher said. "I saw them out there by that altar y'all were just looking at. I don't understand them, I try, but I just don't get it." The preacher shuffled his feet and adjusted his hat.

"Preacher," Virginia said, "imagine if those people tried to convert you to their religion, how long would it take before they convinced you to give up Christianity?" The preacher stood there with a blank look on his face.

"You're absolutely convinced that your religion is the only way to Heaven," she said. "I presume because your culture has been practicing it since the Romans introduced it to your pagan ancestors. You're of English decent, I'm assuming, Jimmy." Jimmy stood there frozen while Virginia went on.

"I imagine that the American Indians in your church are just as sure as you are," she said, "that their spiritual practices are just as correct as yours. But at least they're willing to spend time with Christianity as well." Virginia was trying to judge if the preacher would start yelling again. The preacher stood still looking blankly at Virginia.

"When missionaries first came to the New World they traveled with soldiers who used genocide, brute force, economic gain, political power, or merely survival to persuade the American Indians to practice Christianity," she said. "And many did follow European versions of Christ's teachings eventually. After as many as ninety percent of them died from diseases, sometimes deliberately spread or, worse yet, murdered by the military or settlers for their ancestral lands. Eventually the American military deliberately killed off the remaining buffalo just to starve the Indians onto the reservations."

"At that point it became blackmail-either become a Christian and be protected by the Church or perish. Not really hard to make a decision under those terms, hey, preacher?" Virginia was pushing the argument.

The preacher studied each of the four briefly for a moment as his face continued turning a brighter shade of red. Rocco took a step in between Virginia and the preacher hoping to avoid further conflict.

"Hey, that is what makes America great, right preacher," Rocco said. "I mean everybody has a right to voice their opinion, right, sir?" Rocco was trying to coax him out of his anger. The preacher seamed to relax and stuck both his hands in his pockets.

"Yeah, about everything but politics and religion" declared the preacher. "I haven't had the company of civilized folks in months. Are y'all hungry?" He turned away from Virginia to look at Pim and Johnny, who turned and looked at each other. The thought of food had everyone smiling and nodding in agreement.

They followed the preacher back to the church, entering in through the rounded double, rough-carved wooden front doors. The old church was bigger than it appeared from the outside. The preacher led the group to his living quarters in the back where there was a little kitchen and dining room.

Preacher James brought out several bottles of wine left over from a private Christmas dinner with his family.

"Some of them were Catholic," he explained sheepishly. Soon everyone had forgotten the religious discussion out in the yard. The preacher heated up some frozen TV dinners while Pim used the time to walk around and study the church's simple but sturdy and functional design.

"How long has this church been here?" Pim asked. The preacher turned from the sink to look at Pim and cleared his throat.

"It's one of the oldest Baptist Churches west of the Mississippi," the preacher said. "The Indians have worshiped here since prehistory. They believe it's some kind of sacred site. There's a sacred site about every one-hundred miles, from what I understand." After dinner while everyone was dreading getting back out on the road this late in the day, the preacher observed their half-mast eyes and smiled to himself.

"I don't know if you guys are looking for a hotel or a camp ground," the preacher said. "But you're a heck of a long way from either one. Wouldn't bother me any if you rolled your sleeping bags out on the floor in here or if you got tents you could pitch them outside. Like I said earlier, I miss company."

"I don't know about the rest of them, but it's getting close to sundown," Rocco said. "And that sounds mighty friendly of you, preacher. What do y'all think?" Rocco turned to look at his friends.

Virginia agreed with Rocco, and they all helped the preacher clean up the dinner dishes and put them away. Preacher James, who always loved to preach, talked their ears off while they moved about getting ready for bed.

Virginia suggested to Johnny that he pitch their tent outside. She secretly hoped they might have a chance to take a closer look at the sacred site outside after everyone had gone to sleep.

Johnny pitched the tent near the site hoping it wouldn't be too obvious when they went back and forth during the night just in case anyone was watching. It was nearly midnight when Virginia and Johnny slipped out of the tent. They had each taken a nap on the hard ground waiting for everyone to go to sleep. The humidity was low the sky was clear, and a fair amount of starlight guided them back over the path they had walked earlier in the day. The distance was a little over a quarter of mile from the church. The barren ground had a well-worn trail that presented very few problems in the luminescent night.

As Johnny and Virginia neared the altar site, they heard soft drumming noises, growing louder the nearer they got. Within visual distance of the altar they could see silhouettes of female figures dancing and singing in the moonlight by the flicker of a small fire. They were chanting in their native language wearing traditional dress decorated with colorful beads and trim shining iridescent in the glowing light.

Virginia stopped Johnny by gently placing her hand on his arm and whispered.

"We must not disturb these people," she said. "They are performing a sacred ceremony, to honor the arrival of womanhood for the young girl." Johnny nodded his head showing he understood, refusing to take his eyes off the scene. His strong curiosity about things native over-rode his better judgment that told him he was acting like a peeping tom.

"This is an ancient rite of passage when a girl comes of age," Virginia went on. "The aunts and the mother must hold a ceremony to explain the tribal passage into womanhood, her role, and her duties within the family and the tribe, her place in the circle of life. It teaches the young girl that she will be as one with Mother Earth and will bear children. The children must be reared in a holy manner. The ceremony is a source of much holiness and honor for the new woman and for the whole Indian Nation. It is a turning point in her life. It would be a sin for us to disturb them." Virginia said. She and Johnny turned away from the ceremony, embarrassed to have intruded, even if they were unnoticed.

Halfway back to camp they spotted the preachers silhouette crouched against the night horizon. He was attempting to hide from Virginia and Johnny behind some brush and rocks. They walked up to him smiling at his efforts to spy on them.

"Jimmy, it's awfully late for a walk, don't you think?" Virginia whispered. The preacher stood and gave an uncomfortable sigh.

"I thought I'd follow you two to see what you were doing," the preacher said. "I find the locals out here all the time. What are you guys doing out here, if I may ask?"

"We're interested in the practice of religion-of all kinds," Johnny said. "We are excited about being at this holy site of American Indian spiritual traditions. In fact, Virginia and I are on our way to Taos to talk to an American Indian Shaman. That's their equivalent to you." The preacher was speechless for a moment obviously holding back strong emotion. Slowly he began to talk.

"Why is it that the old ways are still with these people? Even against such overwhelming odds?" the preacher asked. "I've talked to other men of the cloth-you know Christian priest, preachers, even rabbis. Many of them agree that, possibly, there is more than one way to heaven. The preacher continued. I mean who knows? Who really knows, where we all should be headed spiritually? Jesus said that only through Him. Mohammed said only him. I don't believe there is enough time left in the universe to convert all these different groups."

"I don't know, preacher," she said. "But I can tell you, if you want these local people to respect your message, you must respect theirs. You can't dictate a system of personal belief."

"The older I get the more I realize that," Jimmy said and turned walking slowly back toward the church.

"Preacher," Virginia said. "Don't you think it's possible that the Creator wants a diversity of religions just as he wants a diversity of people?" The preacher shrugged his shoulders and continued walking away.

ADVERSE-DIVERSE-PASSIONATE

White Deer had gone into the Four Corners desert to meditate and pray. It was an area where a large civilization of forgotten ancient people had once dwelled. He rarely came to the area and only now because his intuition kept telling him that some great change was taking place in the world. He fasted for three days not knowing what to expect when finally a vision appeared before him. The vision seemed to have something to do with a sudden occurrence or an abrupt shift in the world and of a particular path to follow, a path that all humanity was directed to walk.

White Deer envisioned the world in its entirety, ancient in its beginning and diverse in people, cultures and technology with all of them sharing a common goal, predetermined and wholly agreed upon. Agreed upon by every soul, past, present, and future, even before their common Father, God had created the Earth. A goal shared for and with, the common good of all humanity for a life with no conflicts of interest in the entire universe, a Universe created within spiritual and natural laws all in harmony. White Deer could see many villages all separated by different versions of understanding, belief and worship of the same God.

Worshiping the same God, each with a different way of worship, all based on common universal laws, none being complete by themselves. Given their human limitations of practice and understanding. White Deer believed this was a good thing. He knew that every human had to walk a separate path through life. From birth to the grave, every person was to walk a special path that God created only for him or her, each person complete with the freedom to choose.

He could see that a different system of respecting and worshiping God in each village was an acceptable thing and all parts of a whole. Were they any people from any one village or belief who could ever still their egos and broaden their spirituality sufficiently to know the vastness of God's love and plan for humankind?

Wars and events where humans killed or mistreated each other often were over differences in worship of the same God. Opposing groups like Muslims and Christians in Eastern Europe or Protestant and Catholic Christians in Northern Ireland hating each other, both praying to the same God to help them dominate the other. Though history one dominance was determined, the winner would take all in the name of their loving God, as though they worshiped a different Divine Being. In reality, all practice racial and spiritual bigotry and hatred, not Christianity, in the name of God. The end result is the twisting and distortion of their organized religions to further perpetuate and sanctify their personal ill-gotten gains.

This destructive behavior had been going on since ancient times. White Deer believed there must be a path forward, away from the inhumanity by humanity, a path where peace could rule the world, where peace would subdue the world. Subdue, not through momentary one-sided military dominance but through the worship of the One God, by Whom all life had been created.

Peace would be a achieved not by a one world governmental system, but would be achieved by simply accepting and respecting the right of personal, cultural, and spiritual individuality for all peoples. To refuse to pass judgment or condemn and recognize the need for spiritual diversity, which existed to help diverse peoples find the common salvation. A common salvation that few would completely, wholly know on this earth.

"Wake up in there," Pim said. His voice boomed through thin nylon walls of the domed tent. "We've got a long way to go and plenty of time to get there." Johnny and Virginia sat up wiping the sleep out of the corners of their eyes and stretching.

"I don't think I got enough sleep last night," he mumbled. "I feel like we've been on the road for weeks." His back ached from the hard ground. "I wonder if we'll ever get to Taos." His aching body was giving him second thoughts about being out so long on the road. He didn't realize Pim was still standing outside the tent.

"Well, if you didn't keep a girl in the tent with you, you could get some sleep," Pim smiled. Johnny and Virginia laughed at Pim's comment.

"The only thing keeping me awake in here is Johnny's alligator-like snoring," Virginia said.

Virginia and Johnny crawled out, washed their faces, and packed their motorcycle. Preacher Jimmy prepared a huge breakfast, for which each one of them gratefully thanked him.

"Virginia, I'm going to try looking at my church members with an eye toward a common God," the preacher said. "Keep in touch"

"Preacher, I bet they could be better friends than parishioners. You never know, they might actually start coming to church regularly. Maybe," she said. "anything is possible."

They mounted their bikes and waved goodbye one last time. Las Vegas, New Mexico was on their minds now.

The desert was deathly silent except for Nature's eternal wind-song muted with countless insect, animal, and bird sounds. Johnny hated to push the start button, he felt like it would be disturbing the peace. He scanned the sky for encroaching storm clouds but only saw the patient ballet of slow moving and ever-evolving white cumulus far off in the distance. Pim broke the silence with his engine firing to life.

Johnny waited until last to start his engine, still feeling a little guilty about Rocco almost crashing his bike in the gas station parking lot the day before. Privately, though he laughed at the image of Rocco flapping his arm and chasing his bike around in circles like a circus pony.

Everyone's head was sun burnt from riding without helmets the day before, except for Virginia's whose abundant hair had shielded her scalp. Johnny first noticed the damage when he tried to run a comb through his hair that morning. He figured Rocco and Pim had made similar discoveries. All three of the men had left their helmets handy as they loaded their bikes.

"Rocco, why are you wearing your helmet?" Virginia said. She already had guessed the answer. "Your old bald head ain't sun burnt is it?" Rocco glared back at her. He didn't appreciate references to his age or his appearance he prided himself on being macho.

"Uh, yeah, that's right, my old balding head is so crispy, I can hardly touch it," Rocco said. He swung his leg over the Wide Glide and pulled out the choke. Turning on the ignition, he checked for the neutral light and pushed the start button. Varoom, thump, thump, what an exciting noise! Johnny thought. They pulled away from the little church, Jimmy stood waving as they drove away. He was thinking that nothing ever happens by accident as the dust settled on him.

The three bikes rode down the dirt and stone church driveway. It was similar to dirt track riding, Pim thought, as Rocco dodged the dips and holes all over both sides of the one lane road.

The four of them hit Highway 104 at a fast pace, jockeying for the lead, it was a race to the table-like top of the high plains out on the distant horizon. Now the flat western plain of desert stretched out for miles in front of them. Rising out of the distant haze, a majestic mountain slowly came into view northwest of Truillo.

It appeared to be a ride up yet another hill, although more winding, as they had been doing before, but as they crested the top, they found they had arrived on the base of the legendary High Plains. The hill had led them onto the floor of high mountain plains that western fiction writers had often used for background. Off in the far distance, still hours away, the Sangre De Cristo Mountain Range rose further into the hazy sky.

The sudden and fantastic change in landscape screamed photo opportunity. Pim was the first to slam on his brakes. Each of them took off their helmets, and brushed their hair down onto their sun burnt scalp to pose on their modern-day choppers. Like Old West cowboys, they sat on their iron horses out in the High Plains.

After the first round of photographs, Rocco asked Virginia to sit on the back of his bike to pose with him as Johnny snapped pictures. Virginia politely cooperated with the stunt.

"My wife will love this shot," Rocco said. "I'm going to tell her that early-on Virginia got mad at Johnny and I had to carry her on the back of my bike, almost the entire trip." Rocco laughed so hard Virginia had to help him hold up the bike.

"I better not get any calls from wives about this trip or I will not come along next time," she said.

"You mean if I had been married you wouldn't have ridden with me?" Johnny asked.

"In your case I would have made an exception," she smiled. "But then again, I don't think any woman would have ever been foolish enough to marry you." Everyone roared with laughter Johnny included.

"You know, we're sitting here right in the middle of the road in the turn of this hill," Pim said. "If a speeding vehicle were to come up, we might all be wiped out." Everyone took Pim's statement to heart.

"But then again we haven't seen a car all day." Virginia hopped back on Johnny's bike and Johnny pulled over to the side of the road.

"Hey, Pim, is your back tire low?" Rocco called. Pim looked at the tire and agreed it looked as if it had lost air.

"Oh, crap," Pim said as he got off the bike and started digging for his can of Fix-A-Flat. Johnny got off and walked over to take a closer look. Air was hissing out from around a nail buried in the tire. Johnny slipped his finger over the tiny hole to see if he could feel air rushing out.

"Rocco, let me have your pocket tool," Johnny said and he reached for the tool. "Pim, I'm going to pull out the nail, I can see it right here." Johnny pointed to the spot.

"No, don't," Pim said. "This tire-fix-it stuff may not plug a bigger hole. If I can get it to stop, I'll get it patched in the next town."

Pim connected his can and pressured up the tire. It appeared to be holding so they all took off again hoping to find a service station before it went completely flat. The temperature had dropped with the rise in elevation and they found themselves fastening up the collars and sleeves on their coats.

Bodies ravished and stomachs growling they finally pulled into the small town of Las Vegas and could check on Pim's tire. They had ignored their hunger for hours. The practice of traveling in groups causes individuals to sacrifice personal comforts. Even basic comforts such as hunger and thirst are often ignored for the good of the whole.

They needed a gas station and food. They also wanted to add clothes to their bodies. Johnny figured that afternoon would be the coolest yet of their trip. Rocco in the lead slowed to allow everyone to catch up at a stop sign. There was no traffic at the intersection.

"Where y'all want to eat?" he said.

"I'll eat anywhere," Johnny said. He could smell the kitchen exhaust fan of a nearby restaurant. "What about that place right there." Johnny was pointing to a little brown brick mom-and-pop place on the left side of the road.

"Fine with me," Pim replied. "They've got a gas station right next door so I can check my tire out."

"Rocco," Pim said. "Order me a hamburger, fries and a root beer."

Johnny pulled into the parking lot, his hands were tingling from the ride. His fingers ached when he released the handlebars. His legs were slightly numb from the cool air. His sun burned head was still very tender, as he was reminded when he pulled off his helmet.

"My face is wind and sun burnt," Johnny said. He squinted and relaxed his face to feel the extent of the damage.

"I brought some sun screen," Virginia said. "I'll get it out so you can put it on using the restaurant restroom mirror."

"Thanks. Please remind me to put my chaps on before we leave," he said. "How are you holding up? Are you cold?" He looked at Virginia, genuinely concerned.

"I'm very comfortable behind you," she answered with a smile. "But I think I'll put on an extra shirt before we leave for the afternoon ride." Before they had gotten in the door, Pim came riding up on his FXR wearing a big grin on his face. He parked next to Rocco.

"What did you do with your tire?" Virginia asked after Pim turned off the motor.

"We pulled the nail out and it didn't leak," Pim said. "So I bought another can of tire fix-it stuff." He shrugged his shoulders. "They told me I'd have to pull the tire off myself if I wanted to patch it. So I decided to take a chance."

"They don't do motorcycle tires there?" she asked surprised. Pim shook his head. He didn't talk much, Virginia was beginning to realize.

"Hey, I'm going to get a table," Johnny told the others. "I presume everyone is as hungry as I am?" The four of them nearly raced for the front door, as Johnny took the first step.

Inside the small restaurant there were seven or eight tables but only a few people eating. They were early for the lunch crowd but late for the breakfast crowd. Las Vegas was a small town with a blend of Caucasians, Spanish and American Indians, but the menu was completely southwestern. They discussed their choices.

"We can get hamburgers anywhere," Rocco said. They didn't recognize the breakfast dishes on the menu and Rocco and Pim didn't bring in their reading glasses, as usual, so they couldn't read the menu. A pleasant looking waitress came over to take their orders, Rocco laid his menu down on the table quietly surrendering to his handicap.

"What do you recommend from the menu?" Rocco said. The waitress, guessing his dilemma, suggested that he try the enchiladas and chili. It appeared to be a local favorite as they looked over the other people in the restaurant's plates. All deciding to have the same item off the menu, enchiladas, and chili, the waitress asked if they wanted red or green sauce. No one at their table seemed to know the difference.

"I don't care for a really hot sauce," Pim said to the waitress. "Which one is milder?" She was a little taken aback by the question, not having served tourists very often. She then smiled showing amusement.

"It all depends," she said. She had everyone's attention now and was enjoying the opportunity to be an authority on something other than the daily special.

"Depends on what?" Pim said. The waitress's's smile grew.

"It depends on whose eating it," she said. She gave him a big fully-satisfied grin, obviously taking pleasure from the vague answers she was offering. Pim was at a mental standstill, unable to make a decision with the information available. Virginia broke the deadlock by asking her to bring some of each. The waitress surrendered to Virginia, not wanting her "game" to get in the way of gratuities.

During dinner their four opinions were compared, as to which sauce was hotter, the conclusion was as the waitress had foretold: it all depended on who was eating it.

From Las Vegas they aimed their bikes northward up onto Highway 518. Rocco and Pim decided to stick with the original plan, to head straight for Taos passing through a southern approach. Virginia wanted to revisit an old hotel in a little town named Cimarron and Johnny agreed. Their working relationship with Rocco and Pim had grown strained on the road, as group relationships do. No one was at fault, they each had some personal agenda separate from the group. As long as they had shared their common goals, like the ride out, there had been benefits to the joint experience. However, dividing into smaller groups now made the most sense and they all agreed.

There wasn't a lot to see in the tiny turn-of-the-last-century town of Cimarron although the surrounding landscape was worth the journey all by itself. Once a well-known and traveled watering hole of the last century, the old hotel situated there in the mountain pass had been built in the latter 1800's. At the close of the Indian Wars, at the close of the California Gold Rush, at the close of the Old West finally. Virginia had only mentioned the hotel to Johnny, it had been her only real request on the entire trip. Johnny wanted be sure Virginia had enjoyed the trip. He reckoned that after she introduced White Deer to him, she would go back home to her husband and Naichie.

The historic Saint James Hotel guest book held names like Buffalo Bill, Annie Oakley, Kit Carson, Wild Bill Hitchcock, Bat Masterson, Billy the Kid, and other contemporaries of the age. Some of them had traveled under aliases, some had left tales of their lives, and others bullet holes in the ceiling above the old barroom from shootouts, disputes and bad card hands.

"Buffalo Bill and Annie Oakly once sat in this very dining room and planned their Wild West Show," Debbie said. Debbie, the receptionist, was very friendly and encouraged questions about the historic old hotel and town. "May we have the room Buffalo Bill spent the night in?" Johnny asked. Virginia said nothing but looked around the room as if she were looking for someone. Debbie told them that the room was open and helped carry Virginia's bags up the creaking wooden stairs pointing out the different furnishings original to the old hotel. Historic plaques hung in the hallways telling bits and pieces of local characters and history.

"I got first dubs on the tub," Virginia said. Johnny turned to watch her as she raced him to the bathroom, bag in hand, as soon as Debbie left.

"I could use a hot bath and a good night's rest myself," Johnny said. He laughed out loud at Virginia's rush for the first bath as he sat down on the edge of the bed facing the window. He had been hoping for a moment of privacy to talk on the telephone. Johnny wanted Lee to check on the lottery ticket to make sure it was still safely tucked away on the boat. Johnny picked up the telephone and then sat it back down, reconsidering telling anyone exactly where the ticket was hidden. Although he was worrying about the ticket more every day he spent on the road, he decided against calling.

While Virginia it seemed tried to use up all the hot water in the hotel, Johnny flipped through the tourist information on the tiny desk, daydreaming. Glancing through the original old wavy window glass, he spotted a message scratched on the pane "A. O. loves W. C." and then some small children playing in an empty field across the street. He wondered if Virginia's husband's mind was working and if it was, if he was thinking about Virginia right now.

Opening the window facing the street Johnny lit one of Virginia's cigarettes, inhaling and feeling guilty both for taking a cigarette without asking first and then for smoking it although he told himself it was possibly alright in moderation. He was sure Virginia wouldn't have minded if she knew but he didn't want to interrupt her hot bath to ask. Blowing the smoke out the window into the evening breeze he watched as it moved gently past the window and then quickly up toward the mountains. Chilly air rushed in the room flushing out the warmer air filling the room with the urgency of a late fall day.

After what seemed an hour of hearing only the sound of water dripping in the bathroom, Johnny became worried about Virginia and called to her. He got no answer so he walked to the bathroom door and put his ear to it. He could hear her softly sigh.

"Are you all right?" he said. No answer came back again. He tapped on the door and asked "What's the water dripping so long for?" Virginia's voice responded back through the large six panel heavy wooden door.

"I'm letting the hot water drip to keep the bath warm," she said. Johnny smiled to himself.

"I was worried about you," Johnny said. "I haven't heard from you in a while." He could hear her chuckle quietly to herself.

"Would you mind scrubbing my back?" Virginia said. Johnny's hair stood up on the back of his neck. His first instinct was to ignore her request, to pretend it was never said.

"What did you say?" he asked.

"Would you mind scrubbing my back?" Virginia repeated. He opened the bathroom door slowly, peeking around the edge. Steam clouds rolled out into the bedroom. Virginia was sitting up in the bath tub and had bubbles floating so deep only her head could be seen.

"The hotel provides bubble bath," she said. "I think I used too much in my bath water." He and Virginia giggled like children, their faces blushed red. Johnny didn't notice Virginia blushing because her face was already red from the steaming bath water. Beads of perspiration peppered her face and stands of her long hair lay matted against it.

"But don't worry, I saved you some bubbles," she said. She wore a mischievous smile and nothing more. Johnny could feel his excitement mounting, and it seemed out of place to him now after they had slept next to each other for days.

"Here's a wash cloth," she said. Her polished red fingernails appeared in stark contrast out of the soft white bubbles and a large steaming white wash cloth. "Scrub my back please, if you can find it, that is. I've never had a bubble bath with this many bubbles." She smiled back over her shoulder and leaned forward through the bubbles. Johnny scrubbed.

She leaned her head down onto her slender knees, arms encircled now exposing her creamy back. Johnny took a deep breath and slowly traced the outline of her perfectly formed shoulders. Slipping down the middle of her back along the sides of her arms and again up to her neck, the bubbles rolled away showing more of her. Fetal position, knees to her chest, mashing her barely concealed breast, outward along her thighs, breast on one side of her thighs, calves on the other, Johnny's knees trembled. Ample rounded voluptuous body parts, perfectly formed, and pressed together shined wetly in the low light. Taunt with muscle on the outsides and in the middle soft.

"I used to have a big claw-foot tub like this when I lived in North Carolina," she said. "My husband and I had an old Amish house built in the 1700's. The tub was almost big enough to swim laps in." She laughed her little girl laugh. Johnny finished the back scrub and handed her back the wash cloth, sighing deeply.

"Would you like me to towel you dry?" he said. He wasn't polished at flirting and Virginia ignored him.

"Thank you very much for the back scrub," she said. "I promise to be out soon." Johnny looked around the room for a towel, grabbed one off the cabinet shelf, and sat it next to the tub. He wanted to climb into the tub with her, to hold her, to make promises to her, to win her, to know her. He stepped away from her.

"After two days on the road and no bath last night you deserve to pamper yourself," he told her. "I might just sleep in the thing if you ever get out." She laughed at his corny joke as Johnny walked out of the room gently closing the door behind him, knees trembling.

MEDICINE MAN OF TAOS, NEW MEXICO

Daylight broke through the sheer curtains on the east window of their corner room. A sunbeam leaped off the bright ball as it first radiated above the horizon an eternity away. Awakening Johnny into a semi-conscious dream state, one foot in the dream world and one foot on earth, softness, warmth, and smoothness surrounded him.

His eyelids lay heavy and closed and he wondered into which reality he should step. Aromatic heated smells laced with lavender and freshly washed baby's skin raced through his nostrils fanning his imagination. Not remembering going to bed, falling asleep, or having slept that soundly in a long time, maybe ever. He remembered feeling breathing next to him, no on him. Breathing deep, peaceful, heavy and thick, and slow, and syrupy, slowly heaving, completely in and out, up and down. Rising and falling, refreshing and warm, caressing and soft, touching an ear then a cheek. Moistening his chest with its fertile humidity, settling like dew upon a ripe spring meadow, leaving the chill of anticipation as its cycle rolled in waves again and again.

Surrendered warm, silky, soft, and naked, rounded and tender, perfectly formed and pressed velvety onto toned contour. Swelling and taunt muscles, throbbing, surging, rising to fullness crying for attention.

Mounted, mutual, half-dreaming in, half-waking out, hungry, fearing that any moment consciousness would deliver only a dream or an unwelcome reality.

Plunging, gasping then heaving and clawing to complete and fulfill an utterly magnificent and unstoppable act, milking the last, then frozen, clinched. Overwhelmed at the release of the denied, a thirst quenched. At last he lay sleeping, no longer dreaming.

Forcing an opening, only a tiny slit, he could see how she rested like a little girl, an angel from heaven he thought. Her thick dark hair tossed over the pillow and laying on her rosy cheeks and eyelids. Her strong dark eyebrows carried their perfect arch even while she slept. Deep red lips protruded through the tufts of hair obscenely erotic still. For the first time since the trip had begun, he'd slept a full eight hours.

He replaced his over stuffed feather pillow under his head. She didn't move.

"Why are you staring at me?" Virginia whispered. A self-satisfied smile spread the full width of his suddenly blushing face.

"I, uh, I was just thinking how much you look like a child when you're sleeping," he said. He had wanted to say angel.

"Thank you, I take that as a compliment," she said. Her voice was husky and soft with a morning quality that sounded like a kitten purring. "Would you order coffee to our room while I shower?" She had a joyous child-like happiness in her voice, the kind that makes people believe something exciting was just about to happen or had just happened, when she spoke. Johnny had always heard it, but only now had become conscious of its full beauty. The tones ran from deep to high and back to deep, always in key, like the first songbird of a perfect morning, after a long night of thunderstorms.

"I've got a feeling that today is going to be another one of those unforgettable days," she said. Johnny picked up the telephone on the table by the bed and called the front desk. Virginia wrapped herself in a bed spread and went to the bath.

Debbie the innkeeper, could be heard coming up the squeaky old wooden stairs, one soft slippered footstep tiptoeing after the other. A steaming pot of freshly brewed coffee could be smelled well before her arrival. Johnny cracked open the door before she arrived and jumped back into bed, he could have laid there hours more.

"I hope you don't mind, but I brought you guys the whole pot of coffee," Debbie said. She pushed through the partially opened door. Johnny smiled brightly with blankets pulled up to his chin.

"Thanks," he said. "What's the occasion?"

"Oh, I guess you caught me on a good day and besides, we haven't started breakfast," Debbie said. "I didn't figure you guys would want to wait?" Johnny smiled back at her, she had a personality he couldn't help but like. Debbie obviously liked everyone.

"Thanks, and you're right, we've got to move on to Taos," he said. "We're going to see a friend of Virginia's today."

Debbie set the coffee down on the dresser and walked over to the window partially opening the curtain. She turned smiling at Johnny again before walking back to the coffeepot. Virginia was sitting up in her bed leaning back against her large feather pillow brushing her wet hair. Debbie motioned to Virginia asking her what she wanted in her coffee.

"Cream and sugar," Virginia said. Debbie handed her the steaming cup with the spoon still in it.

"Do you take sugar or cream?" she asked. Johnny completed his yawn slowly and looked back at her.

"Black please," he said. "I wanted to ask you about those old land grants I saw framed and posted down there in your hallway museum." Debbie smiled back at him. She was the local historian, an honorary position that had come with the title of innkeeper. She took pleasure in answering her guest's questions.

"What about them?" she said.

"I noticed the government, a long time ago was giving away large land grants," he said. "Some over a million acres to private individuals?" Debbie handed Johnny his coffee.

"You've got to realize how big America is or once was," Debbie said. "My husband works with the Federal Bureau of Land Management and I've asked him the same question. Did you realize that one third of America, mostly in the West and Alaska, is still unused Federal land?" Johnny didn't believe what he was hearing.

"In the beginning America's founding fathers' intentions were to give all the land away to settlers as quickly as possible," Debbie said. "That was the fastest way of keeping the unsettled territory out of the hands of other foreign colonial powers. They carried out that plan until the turn of this century. Then the Federal Government stopped for some reason. I guess the threat of foreign colonial powers had subsided."

"You sure seem to know a lot about United States history," Johnny said trying to encourage her to go on. Johnny took a sip of black coffee and Virginia gently stirred the sugar and cream into her coffee, gently, listening and thinking.

"What gave them the right to take land from the native peoples?" Virginia finally said. She set the spoon back on the serving tray next to her bed. Debbie smiled at them both. She loved an interested audience.

"You know, that was never Thomas Jefferson's full plan," Debbie said. "He wanted to save the lands west of the Mississippi River for the American Indians. Jefferson hoped to bring them into the democracy as valuable trading partners, harvesters of the wilderness. But instead they were destroyed by wave after wave of European settlers." Johnny sat waiting for Virginia to comment, but she didn't. Debbie wished him and Virginia good luck on their journey and they thanked her for the coffee before she left the room.

Virginia slowly packed her bags, neither one of them saying much of anything to the other. There was something disturbing about what Debbie had said that was bothering both of them. Although neither of them could put their finger on exactly what it was. Then, at the same time, they turned and looked at each other, their eyes lit up.

"How could something this big have been neglected for so long?" she wondered out loud. "The United States is holding stolen lands, one third of the country is sitting virtually unused, It needs to be returned to the rightful owners." Discussing the new information while they packed, the questions on each of their minds was why hadn't the unused lands been returned to the rightful and proper owners, and could they start the process?

"America, the world's greatest democracy, the foremost human rights leader, or so it seems, was in all reality a living lie." Johnny said. "America sent tens of thousands of young men to their deaths in Vietnam to stop the Communist North from taking over the democratic people of the South."

"America was willing risk its military people to stop Saddam Hussein from gaining control over the people of the Middle East. America was willing to send troops into Eastern Europe to stop the modern-day genocide there. America even labeled China and other countries human rights violators."

"Why isn't America giving back the unused lands it took from the American Indians?" Virginia questioned. "Tell me. Tell me why the President of the world's greatest democracy has pushed through legislation to prohibit entry into the United States of any person or company who profited from confiscated lands in Cuba?" Johnny gave Virginia a blank look. "You know, any lands that Castro's government stole from Cuban refugees now living in the United States." Johnny shrugged his shoulders.

"Frankly, I haven't paid that much attention to international politics," Johnny said.

"But the President is standing on stolen American Indian land" she said, "pointing his finger at other human rights violators."

"Stolen property," he said. He was thinking now. "Virginia, you know the United Nations is finally calling for the Swiss Government to force the Swiss banks to give up the monies and properties stolen from the Jews in World War II. Do you think we could work with the United Nations to give back unused Federal lands to the American Indians, the rightful owners?"

"You're crazy, JT," she said, but she liked the thought of doing something, anything. For Johnny even to suggest something was to be done, or even could be done made her shiver with excitement.

"Yeah, all the girls tell me that," he joked and Virginia shook her head smiling.

"You'll never get away with it," Virginia's feeling was quickly changing to panic. "They'll destroy you, if not kill you, Johnny. You don't realize what you be up against? It's not just a bureaucratic problem it's racism, it's greed, it's ignorance, it's hate."

Johnny picked up the telephone by the bed and dialed Lee. Virginia watched him breathlessly wondering what in the world he could possibly have in mind, let alone who he might be calling.

"Basically I believe it's a religious problem," Johnny said. Virginia stared blankly.

"Hello," a tired voice answered on the other end of the telephone line. Virginia feigned to check her bag, repacking a few things as she listened to one side of the conversation.

"Lee, this is Johnny, I know you like to sleep late in the mornings, but I wanted to catch you before you left the house," he said.

"JT-where the hell are you and what time is it?" Lee said. "I thought you had gotten kidnaped or something." Johnny laughed out loud into the receiver. He cut his eyes over to Virginia and their eyes met in a meaningless glance.

"I called you last night and your answering machine wasn't even on," Johnny said, an exaggeration because Johnny hadn't waited long enough for an answering machine to pick up.

"I'm not kidding," Lee said. "I've been calling everywhere looking for you. Karen and I have been worried sick about you. Are you all right?"

"Fine, thanks," Johnny said.

Control persons couldn't help themselves and instinctually found some means to maintain control. It was their comfort zone, both a talent and a curse. Powerful people always had the trait because it brought them whatever they sought with great consistency. Johnny had always seen it and had often appeared to give in easily to keep the peace. Resisting was a constant chess game. Having developed certain defenses such as explaining only the bare minimum, a working friendship had developed.

Many more people were charmed by those control personalities than were offended. Typically, those who tolerated control were of two basic types. There were those with little self-confidence who found comfort in being controlled, making few decisions by themselves was appealing. Then those with a great deal of self-confidence, who would let others run the show and do all the planning toward a common goal. Of those in the self-confident category, they controlled through subtle manipulation non-confrontational style. Not meaning that anyone could be blind to manipulation, but it was strength also and respected in other people. Much like a code of ethics for lawyers if all such things were not oxymorons.

The odd thing was that those personalities of low self-esteem, those who easily surrendered control of their lives and liberties to persons of a control nature, were eventually destroyed and disposed of. Even when the dependant personality can devote life's energies to being directed by another person, many control persons lacking spiritual depth lost respect for dependant persons. Like a cat that tires of batting a mouse around, the cat finally loses interest, killing the mouse with a quick snap of its jaws. As a predator the cat never reaches a state of peace or harmony and is always hunting or digesting its last kill.

Lee and Johnny talked for half an hour before Johnny caught him up on everything that had been going on with the trip, then apologized again for waking him up so early.

"The time zone," Johnny said. "I didn't think about the time zone," Lee told Johnny, Lee needed to get up early anyway for a tee-off at Mallard Cove. The district attorney was trying to win back last week's loss.

"Lee, could you run a search on the Internet for me, to see what you could find on the United Nations," Johnny said. "Anything on work going on to get back the Nazi plunder from World War II or Cuban land seizures in Castro's regime. I'll call back in a few days to see what you've found." Lee was too drowsy to question Johnny about reasons behind his strange request. He just agreed and went back to sleep.

Virginia and Johnny mounted the white Harley Davidson then waved goodbye to Debbie who waved goodbye from the herb garden inside the white adobe garden wall. Johnny cranked the bike and pulled out of Cimarron as quietly as possible, so as not to disturb the tiny village.

They headed north toward the snow-capped mountains and west toward the artist community of Taos, New Mexico. Their bike eagerly climbed into the mountains. The scenery changed dramatically as though stepping back into the previous season. Spots of frozen snow lay in shady areas of the upper elevations. Johnny slowed the bike, maneuvering the winding switchbacks while he torque-happy Harley peacefully idled. Virginia saw an opportunity to talk to Johnny as they passed huge shear, jagged rocky cliffs rising several hundred feet into the air abutting the road.

"It's breathtaking," she said.

"I believe the roadside sign called them palisades," Johnny said. "They appear to be rock cliffs shoved straight out of the ground, hundreds of feet up." Johnny wondered what would happen to Virginia and him once they reached Taos.

The ancient city of Taos sat in a bowl, a crater surrounded by fortress like mountains, secluded as though they were entering some privileged Shangri-La. They diminished slowly down into the city amazed at all the colors and options and diversions a civilization can provide but one doesn't notice unless they have been deprived. The natural mountain surround had served the native Taos population well many years ago. The mountains kept out the first waves of European explorers and immigrants, their devastating diseases and disastrous hungers for the accumulation of land and wealth. Johnny was amazed at the wide and varied use and colors on the adobe structures now commercialized and all neatly painted shades of pastels and off whites.

"Where do you want to get some lunch?" Johnny said over his shoulder. "I'm starving."

Virginia comfortably leaned on Johnny while they rode, each offering comfort and support to the other while balancing the bike.

"Out Back," she said.

"What," he said. "Out back of what?" Virginia smiled at Johnny's tumult never knowing when he was cracking a joke.

"Just keep going straight," she said and directed him down the main road to a little pizza place called the "Out Back Restaurant." It was slightly off the main street and out back of another building, still easily visible from the street.

"You'll either love or hate their pizza," she said. "It's not like any pizza you've probably ever tasted before."

The place was set up like a hippie quasi yuppie micro brewery pizza joint. Local children displayed their elementary art on the walls. Rough unfinished wood walls and floors gave it a cabin feeling. The local customers appeared to be artists and shop owners hanging out, talking about their works in progress.

Johnny and Virginia sat at a small table near the entrance, ordered a large veggie pizza and two beers. Johnny was afraid of what it would taste like, veggies and pizza seemed incompatible to him. Nevertheless they were served an excellent lunch, washing it down with some English ale, finally beginning to relax for the first time that day. The apprehension of the trip was slowly dissipating and the realization that they finally had reached their destination was sinking in, while post goal depression hovered on the horizon.

"Virginia, where is this White Deer medicine man fellow anyway? Is he expecting us?" Johnny said. He gulped down his first beer and tried to talk and chew at the same time, he wasn't sure if Virginia understood him.

"Yes, he's expecting us-on Indian time," she replied. She gave him a pizza sauce grin and sipped her beer.

"Indian time," he said. "Is that like Greenwich Mean Time?" She laughed so loud that people turned to look. Johnny laughed along with her. They were both elated to be in Taos and were easily cheered.

"I called White Deer a few days before you began your trip and told him you were coming to visit," Virginia said. "In the American Indian culture, time is not thought of in the same sense as in the popular culture."

"Time is not something you own," she said. "Time is not something to be sectioned, manipulated, or allotted. Time is something that moves us from point to point in our lives, but not in a linear sense, in a circular sense. Time tells people when things began and stopped, not people telling time."

"One of the great faults of the non-aboriginal culture is the belief that ownership superseded all else," she said. "Like man's interest comes before God's, like a spoiled child who believes that parents exist for the use and enjoyment of the child."

"Many non-aboriginal cultures selfishly grab everything they can," she said, "believing that God and His gifts exist for the use and benefit of mankind, that God exists to serve man."

"You've heard those evangelists on television. They flaunt their wealth on stages in front of the cameras," she said, "in front of their followers, the very people who gave them the money. Then they have the gall to tell the poor suckers: 'If you'll only listen to me and do what I say, God wants you to be rich like me. Y'all know the bible tells us so, everybody could be rich if they would only follow its teachings.' People fall for that hokey," she said ."The weak, confused, greedy, lost, trusting, all kinds of people fall for that. They call themselves Christians and claim to follow

Jesus Christ, but in reality they're Hypochristians. Jesus Christ never pursued wealth, not in his entire short life. In fact, Jesus was persecuted by materialistic people of the same sort as the evangelist."

"Jesus was a poor man from a poor home and never tried to fit into the establishment-the establishment hunted him down and crucified him for speaking the truth."

"Jesus Christ's message was love and the forgiveness of sins," she said. "And he taught correct living and thinking. These Hypochristians talk out of both sides of their mouths. They preach from the New Testament when it serves them. Then they jump back to the Jewish books, the Old Testament when it's convenient and serves them."

"Hypochristians believe they will soil themselves if they associate with poor Christians or non Christians," she said. "They huddle together at their Sunday Schools gossiping about each other, especially whoever didn't show up, somehow believing they will go to Heaven because of their self professed goodness. They mistakenly believe that if you live a godly life, God will see to it that you at least live a middle class life."

Johnny looked around checking to make sure no one was listening. Talk like this was heresy in some circles. People could get awfully offended, even if it was often true.

"That reminds me of something that happened when I was a little boy," he said. "I had some cousins who were Christians but not Catholic, and I was really worried about them because at the Catholic school I attended we were being taught that if a person wasn't Catholic they couldn't get into Heaven. This weighed heavily on me for a long time. Finally, gathering courage, I asked my mother what the difference was between the Christian religion of my cousins and our Catholic religion. She was normally a person of few words and conservative beliefs but she could see my concern and being a loving person she wanted to lighten my burden.

"The two religions are very similar," she said. "The only major difference between them and Catholics is that they go out of town to drink and dance."

"This amused me to great ends," Johnny said. "Being just in upper elementary school, we didn't talk about such things, especially with adults. I think that one moment of humor and honesty opened up a line of communication between my mom and me that lasted the rest of her days."

"Hey, you know why a Catholic never takes less than two Baptists fishing with him?" Virginia said. Johnny looked around to see if anyone else was listening.

"No, why?" Johnny said. Virginia could hardly talk she was smiling so widely.

"Because two Baptists don't drink nearly as much of the Catholic's beer as one Baptist does," Virginia said. They both muffled their guffaws and then a voice spoke behind them.

"Hey, I represent that remark," the waitress said. All three looked at each other, giggling like co-conspirators.

They both agreed in the future to keep from making fun of anyone's beliefs. The last thing either of them wanted to alienate anyone or to be a hypocrite. Most people accepted their parents' religious beliefs and were genuinely sincere, even if they were fallible in their practice.

After they had finished the pizza and tipped the young waitress, Virginia suggested that they pass by the Harley Davidson shop down the street, and Johnny eagerly agreed. There is this desire by most Harley riders while on vacation to tour Harley Davidson shops in the towns they pass through. To browse the bikes and to at least buy a souvenir te-shirt.

"It isn't a real Harley Davidson dealer," she said. "It's an 'after market' shop that specializes in Harley Davidson's."

"That's enough," Johnny said. "I need an oil change."

They headed down the main street toward the town square. Retail shops of all kinds lined both sides of the road, evidence of the artist community that had declared it a sacred spiritual site of nature. The faddish overt commercialism reminded Johnny of the French Quarter in New Orleans, a sacred site of the roman god Bacchus. Virginia pointed to a sign down the road on the left. "Doctor Zen's Cycle Shop," the orange and black hand-painted sign announced. They pulled into the parking lot and stopped, there wasn't a single car or bike. The shop appeared closed down, but the lights were on inside.

Johnny opened the unlocked door for Virginia and stepped inside behind her into the showroom. There were racks of clothes, leather jackets, custom bike supplies hanging on the walls, and a guy snoring on the couch. He had a long nearly gray beard and even longer graying hair. The door chimed as it closed behind Johnny and Doctor Zen, an ancient hippie, looked up from his nap.

"Can I help you people?" he asked politely without moving, one eye raised to half-mast.

"I need an oil change," Johnny said. "How long will it take?" Doctor Zen slowly began to sit up now, half way, and told Johnny that they probably had a mechanic back in the shop, he'd check if Johnny wanted him to, then changed his mind.

"But he's fairly busy," Zen said. "You can go back there and ask him if you'd like?" Without waiting for an answer from Johnny, Zen laid his head back down on the couch. Then he spoke again with both eyes closed, "He might be able to help you," finally closing the conversation, his rheumy eyes sealed.

"If I could just get some oil, an oil filter, and a place to dispose of my old oil," Johnny said. "I could do it myself." Doctor Zen finally climbed slowly off the couch and walked to the counter to fulfill Johnny's request. He rang up the sale, took the cash, and told Johnny to pull his bike around the back into the shop and to dispose of his oil in the black drum. Johnny went outside and drove his bike into the small workshop then leaned the bike on its kickstand.

He looked at the black 55-gallon barrel that Zen had said was the waste oil drum and grabbed a dirty rag sitting on nearby bench.

Twisting the oil filter wrapped with the dirty rag he tried to loosen the filter and was having no luck.

"Filter wrench is on the counter behind you," said the mechanic.

Johnny spun around trying to not show his surprise, he hadn't heard anyone come in. "Funnels hanging on the wall to your right."

At first, Johnny hadn't noticed the mechanic working on a bike in the back, and he had been too busy to take notice of Johnny. His hair was long, black, and tied in a ponytail. He wore a black and orange t-shirt that said Harley Davidson, old oil stained blue jeans, and a well-worn pair of slip-on steel toe boots.

"Thanks," he said. "My name is Johnny, people just call me JT, though." Johnny hoped he didn't look too spooked.

"WD's my name. People call me WD-Forty cause I use the stuff on everything," the mechanic related, then went back to his own work. Johnny got the filter and plug off his motorcycle, and while the oil drained he tried to start a conversation.

"A friend and I just rode in from Louisiana," Johnny said. WD kept working, unimpressed as though people from Louisiana come through the shop all the time.

Virginia came through the shop doors.

"I have looked at everything in the show room and didn't find anything I can't live without," she said. "Do you need any help?"

The mechanic turned around looked at Virginia, and stood up. Johnny didn't like the way he stared at Virginia.

"I was wondering when you'd get here," WD said and Virginia smiled back. Johnny's mouth dropped open.

"Let me guess what WD stands for," Johnny said. Virginia and WD chuckled as WD walked over and shook Johnny's hand. Virginia leaned over and kissed WD on the cheek.

"How is Michael?" WD said. Virginia stared into his eyes without saying a word, without blinking. A tear welled up and rolled down her face. WD stepped forward and hug her with just his arms trying not to get any grease on her. He whispered into her ear.

"I wish I could do something to help him, he was always my favorite little brother." For the first time Johnny realized that Virginia and WD were in-laws. Virginia sobbed with deep shaking emotion holding onto White Deer. Johnny finally realized the pain she had courageously kept to herself. Silently he stood by watching them cry on each other's shoulder and secretly he wished Virginia had confided in him more deeply. Perhaps, it would come with time, he thought, things like that come with time.

Johnny picked up his tools and washed his hands while WD and Virginia caught up on family matters, finally they turned to Johnny.

"I didn't expect to find you in a Harley Davidson shop working on motorcycles," Johnny said. "I guess I expected you to be living in a tepee somewhere."

"Hey, a guy has got to feed himself," WD said. "You guys going to stay at my place?" WD looked at Virginia waiting for a reply. Virginia and Johnny looked at each other.

"I don't mind either way," Johnny said.

"That's good idea," she said. "Thank you for the invitation, we'll take you up on it."

"Yeah," Johnny said. "It beats the heck out of sleeping on the ground." Virginia laughed at Johnny.

"You guys have lunch yet?" WD asked.

"Yes, we did," Virginia said. "I treated Johnny to a veggie pizza." Johnny nodded his head in agreement.

"Not bad for a veggie pizza either," Johnny said then belched. They all laughed.

RABBIS AND MEDICINE MEN

Virginia and Johnny followed WD behind the shop to see his bike, a 1955 Pan Head. WD proudly announced that he'd been riding the bike for over thirty years and that it had once belonged to his father. Pearl white paint glowed on its vintage sheet metal. Except for a light road film from the snow that had fallen a few days ago, the bike appeared in showroom condition. WD sat on the seat and kick started the engine once. It fired off. For Johnny, it was love at first sound.

"Johnny, you and Virginia follow me," WD said. Johnny and Virginia climbed aboard the FXR and started it in the shop. Noise echoed off the walls. They pulled past Doctor Zen, who had been awakened out his near coma by the noise and stumbled out to see what was going on, he waved feebly as they left. WD led them past the Taos Indian Pueblos leaving town, heading up the curving mountainous roads that seemed to be taking them north, the best that Johnny could tell. The three of them rode until the black top ran out, then turned left and continued for a mile or two further along a well-groomed dirt and stone road. WD pulled around a large bolder into a yard with a barn, turning off his engine before coasting through the open barn doors, Johnny, and Virginia did the same and pulled up beside him.

The barn had three stalls on either side and what looked like a finished hayloft on top. Horses whinnied from the outside corral WD used to feed and capture the horses when he needed them. Pointing, WD asked Virginia to go to the feed room to pour a gallon of feed into each of the stalls. The horses grunted and chatted to Virginia in their horse talk. Then WD set the barn doors closed and opened the door to the corral. Six large horses trotted into the barn and to their respective stalls. WD introduced the six horses as they munched on their high protein sweet feed. WD was beginning to wonder if he should suggest to Johnny and Virginia that they begin preparations for the Stone Lodge ceremony now.

"Johnny, you guys feel like going for a little hike, before I show you around the cabin?" WD asked. He walked around to the tack room and took out a couple of empty feed sacks while Johnny consulted with Virginia.

"Yeah sounds great WD. We've been sitting on this bike for days-a good hike might help straighten out my back," he answered. WD walked over and handed each of them a sack and a knife.

"Good we need to collect some fresh sage and dried cedar for our Sweat Lodge ceremony," WD said. The three of them walked out to the corral and through the gate. They followed a well-worn path toward the hills. While they walked WD told them about local history and Virginia and Johnny politely listened.

"This is part of the Taos Indian Reservation," WD said. "For more than a thousand years the Taos people have protected and cared for these lands, hundreds of miles around here. The Taos lived in the same village and adobe houses for over nine hundred years. Finally forced off ancestral lands by the settlers, they were only able to hang onto their pueblos until recently."

"These people were hunted and enslaved as were most aboriginal people around the world, even into the 1900's. White people today think that those things happened in ancient times. But there are people alive today who saw those things," WD said.

"Taos children were taken by force to boarding schools, away from their parents. Organized religions and the Federal Government's plans to destroy the American Indian cultures have not been a total success though. Many Indians hung onto their ancient beliefs and customs despite their planned extinction."

"It's really hard to believe," Johnny said. "In our present era of civil rights, equal rights, human rights, children's rights, laws protecting the rights of animals, that the Native Americans are still denied their rights." Virginia and WD nodded in agreement and WD continued up the path.

"Twenty five years ago," WD said. "A U.S. Senator named Redhead, told these people they had to prove the surrounding lands belonged to the tribe before the government would give back to the tribe any of their ancient lands. This Senator believed that proof would never be conclusive. However, the Taos elders hired some archaeologist and proved the camp sites in the hills did belong to the Taos ancestors. So the Senator was forced to keep his word and returned 80,000 acres to the tribe." Virginia and Johnny cheered the ending of WD's story and their arrival at WD's harvest area. They had not spent that much time on their feet all week.

WD showed Johnny and Virginia where he cultivated his sage and asked them to harvest a third of a sack. He then turned to a fallen cedar log nearby, gathered twigs and small branches from the trunk and put them into his bag. The three of them slowly wandered around looking at the native flora while WD identified edible and medicinal plants.

"Where's the Sweat Lodge?" Johnny asked. WD turned and pointed up further toward the hills with his walking staff.

"It's several more miles into the hills," WD said. He lowered his staff and looked at Johnny. "We will have to ride the horses there tomorrow, I hope you can ride?" Johnny nodded his head and told them about the horse that his father had given him as a young boy. The horse had been only two years old and had never been ridden. Under the supervision of his father Johnny tamed and broke the horse over a year or two. WD laughed at the colorful description Johnny gave of the many times the horse had bucked him off and of the adventures in the woods around his uncle's house. They arrived back at WD's barn a little after dark.

"Is your cabin near here?" Johnny asked.

"Yeah, right here," WD said pointing at the barn. Johnny looked around thinking he had missed something then followed WD back into the barn stall area. WD flipped open a cigarette lighter and lit an ancient looking kerosene lantern hanging by a nail on the wall and pointed to the stairwell.

"Right up there," WD said. Johnny and Virginia had presumed a hayloft lay over the first floor of the barn. WD stepped forward holding the lantern high and led them up the stairs as the orange light flickered off the walls on the rough wooden steps. WD opened a hand-hewn door and revealed a beautiful cedar wood paneled living area with the bathroom being the only room separated from the main living area.

"I don't have 110 volt electricity or natural gas," WD said smiling. "But I get along all right without them." Virginia looked at Johnny bewildered. By this time Johnny could read her thoughts and shrugged his shoulders.

"I guess that rules out taking a hot bath?" she said. WD and Johnny laughed at her question, WD explained the cabins water system.

"The black gutter you pointed to out on the roof captures water off one side of the roof that is painted black," WD said. "It goes into a black cistern that acts as a heat bank to gather and hold the sun's radiant heat. The other side of the tin roof is painted white and it collects water in a white cistern, that's our cold water." Virginia nodded without blinking trying to comprehend all that was being said.

"I have solar panels mounted on the black side, which is the south side of the roof. A bank of batteries stored down in the barn in a large vented plastic storage box," WD said. "All the lights in the cabin are 12 volts, so I don't need a converter to get to 110 volts."

"Just like my sail boat," Johnny said. Virginia was trying to grasp all the technical details and stood motionless listening to the two men discuss the smaller details.

"That's not all," WD said. "I've got a looped grid of black hoses on the black roof. During the day when the sun is shining, a separate solar panel runs a tiny D.C. motor. That circulates the water out of the black cistern and through the black hose. This further collects as many BTUs from the sun as possible, then it goes back to the cistern. I've also got an iron pipe that passes in the top of the chimney and runs down into the fireplace and back to the bottom of the black or white cistern to heat water in the winter. The water pressures not so great but it works."

"Where do you get your firewood to heat the place?" Johnny asked.

"Off the lands around me," WD said. "I only harvest sick or dead trees like that cedar we harvested today."

WD hadn't eaten breakfast or lunch, and he figured his guests were at least half as hungry as he. He opened his 12 volt powered ice chest and pulled out some trout he had caught that morning.

"There's a mountain lake not far from here," WD explained. "Only a five minute walk." It was his habit on fair days to fish for breakfast and if it was a good morning, he would have enough for dinner too. That particular morning had been a great morning and he had caught a string of big fish.

WD fired up his wood stove, while Johnny filleted the fish. Virginia rolled them in cornmeal and seasoned them with sea salt and black pepper. WD fried the fillets in olive oil, he didn't think to ask his guests if they liked fish figuring everyone did.

After dinner, they sat around the natural light of a small fire in the freestanding fireplace. In the middle of the room they made prayer ties, little sacks of colorful cotton cloth stuffed with gifts to the spirits and tied at the top with a piece of colorful string.

In the days past before non-aboriginal people had killed all the buffalo prayer ties had been made of buffalo skin. The buffalo had once roamed over nearly the entire United States. Buffaloes were considered sacred to the Indians. Used them for food, housing, clothing, and tools, they were essential to survival.

Sleep came easy to all three of the seekers that night. There were no sounds of civilization, no bumps in the night from traffic or neighbors, only nature and the livestock below them in the barn.

Sometime in the early morning hours, an hour or so before daylight, WD woke and started the process of providing breakfast. Johnny opened one eye as WD moved silently around the cabin.

"Going fishing?" Johnny asked half sleeping, in a state of semi-consciousness.

"Yeah, you interested?" WD replied. He could barely see Johnny in the darkness.

That's all it took to rouse Johnny, He was no fisherman, but the thought of lying in bed for another hour or so, waiting for the sun to rise was less attractive than waiting for fish to bite. The two men quietly slipped though the barn barely waking the horses.

Taking the same well-worn trail they'd used yesterday afternoon, they veered right at the cedar log and arrived at a lakeshore still covered with early morning fog. Frogs and insects leaped out of the way as they edged near the bank and set down their fly-fishing tackle. Crickets chirped so loudly and in such large numbers, it was hard for Johnny to believe possible. WD reached into his vest pocket and unhooked two flies of similar shape but different colors. One was made of red fox fur and white duck down feathers. The other was black and white skunk fur with red bird feathers, WD handed Johnny the skunk fur fly.

"Ever fly fish before?" WD asked, in a hushed voice. It was odd to hear a human voice in the darkness, and it startled Johnny.

"Once back at Boy Scout camp when I was a kid," he answered.

"Just do what I do," WD said. Johnny followed WD movements. WD tied the bait on and pulled enough slack in the line to begin popping the bait in and out of the water beginning next to a small stump near the shore, Johnny tried to follow the motions and wound up tangling the line around himself. Virginia giggled from the brush behind them.

"What the hell!" Johnny said whirling around. He spotted Virginia sitting on a rock only a few feet behind him and WD. She was calmly smiling.

"You trying to scare me into the lake?" Johnny said, he was obviously unnerved.

"No, that mountain lake is probably too cold to go swimming in. I'm just trying to make sure you guys catch us some breakfast," Virginia replied. "Give me that rod." Virginia said, standing. That was all it took to discourage Johnny from fishing that morning or any morning for that matter. Johnny surrendered the offending equipment and took over Virginia's seat on the rock preparing to duck when she back cast. After observing her long enough to be comfortable with her skill level, he asked for one of her cigarettes to ward off the encroaching hunger in his stomach.

Johnny observed the rising sun's reflection on the smooth as glass lake. Birds awoke from their overnight perches and one by one echoed their chorus of songs across the lake's surface commemorating the new day as though it was their last one and all they expected from their Creator. Fish began to leap out of the water, suddenly and instantly as if awaken by a predator or the promise of breakfast, insects began to buzz through the fragrant mountain air. Bees buzzed by, skimming the water's surface for a drink of cool clean water.

Before Johnny had taken the last drag off the cigarette, both Virginia and WD had landed a flopping fish. WD's fish was large enough to feed all three of them for breakfast, he proclaimed. Moments later they were heading back to the barn with three dripping fish in the cool mountain air. There was a car in the clearing by the barn when Johnny, WD, and Virginia got back from fishing. Standing out front was the Native American woman Johnny remembered singing in the Big Texan and a bearded man in dark clothes. Virginia walked up to the woman and the man and they introduced themselves to WD and Johnny. The man was

Rabbi Paul, he had come west to study similarities between the Jewish and the American Indian religions. The woman was Little Feather.

"Virginia," Johnny asked. "How did they know where WD lives and when to meet us here?"

"I called Little Feather, while you and WD were talking in the shop yesterday," she said.

"I didn't know her name was Little Feather?" Johnny said. Virginia smiled back at him.

"It's just a nickname," Virginia said. "You couldn't pronounce her Indian name."

Virginia volunteered to clean up the breakfast dishes while WD and Johnny moved gear from the bikes onto the horses. Rabbi Paul and Little Feather helped Virginia then walked down to the horses. WD figured they would be away only one night but said they should pack for two just in case. From his smokehouse a few yards from the corral he chose some freshly smoked venison and fish and packed it into his saddlebags.

"We should have enough food for a few days," WD said. "Water we can get from the mountain stream that feeds the sacred lake." They each fed their horse a handful of feed and petted them to develop a little rapport before they climbed into their saddles and headed off north again along the trail. This time when they came to the fallen cedar tree and the sage patch, they rode past them.

WD took the lead and after a few hours of non-stop riding they finally stopped at a clearing near a creek where water tumbled noisily over rocks and boulders. The horses noisily slurped on the cool melted snow. In the clearing an old fire pit was encircled by rocks, WD instructed them to set up their tents between the campfire area and the creek. The spring warmth had begun melting the accumulation of winter ice and snow on the upper parts of the mountain.

"Got any fish in there?" Johnny called to WD.

"Yeah, this creek feeds the lake where we caught breakfast," WD said.

After they got the campsite settled, WD led them on a short hike to a circular, windowless adobe structure about 20 to 30 feet in diameter with the entrance on top.

"This is the prayer lodge," WD said. "It is very old and only a few in the tribe still know of its existence. Most of the tribe knows that it is out here somewhere, but only a few of the elders still know its exact location. Some of the elders say that this was the site of their village before the time of Christ. However, the tribe moved to its present location down at the Taos Pueblo over a thousand years ago. No one remembers why. Once a year a secret society of elders comes up here to apply fresh mud to the structure and to pray to the Spirits."

Johnny asked to go inside and look around but WD said it was not allowed.

"Only with a Shaman should you go in, and for religious purposes or if you're seeking protection. We are not quite ready for the ceremony yet," WD said and instructed everyone to return to the camp.

"Relax, meditate and pray the rest of the day," WD said. "Try to avoid taking any food after lunch and then to drink water only. I'll remain at the Sweat Lodge and prepare for the ceremony this evening."

He asked them to come back at sundown but not to enter the Sweat Lodge until the sun had completely dipped below the horizon.

Johnny was more apprehensive than Virginia was. She had attended Sweat Lodges before. Johnny had long hoped to become knowledgeable of Indian ways ever since the day his mother told him of his heritage. Now the time had come and he was afraid reality wouldn't match his expectations or possibly he wouldn't comprehend its meaning. He had grown up in a French culture, not an aboriginal one.

Many years ago while on vacation he'd made an effort to find a reservation and locate the Medicine Man. He told the Medicine Man that he knew there were many things he would not understand, being raised as a Christian. However, he hoped the Medicine Man would explain the Indian religious teachings to him.

The Indian Medicine Man rebuffed him and told him those things he could never know because he was not of their tribe. Moreover, that since he had more European blood than Indian he could never fully understand and should not be bothered with it. Johnny accepted the old man's opinion for a few years believing he was forever caught in the middle of the two cultures, a half-breed. However, eventually his search resumed, realizing he could never stop his desire to know.

BENEVOLENT VISION

The four of them climbed up the rough-hewn timber Sweat Lodge ladder. They had hardly spoken all day and still they said nothing. Now outside on top of the ancient sun baked, mud brown adobe the four of them watched the sun slip behind the surrounding mountain tops. Virginia reached over and grabbed Johnny's hand.

"Johnny, don't worry about the ceremony," Virginia said. Trust me when I tell you the connection to these people that you know in your heart is real. You do belong here. You're not a half-breed without a cultural home roaming the earth with no place to belong," she said. Johnny sighed and wiped the corner of his eye.

"Virginia, do I wear a sign on my forehead telling you what I'm thinking?" he asked. They looked into each other's eyes and climbed down the hand-hewn timber ladder stairs following Little Feather and the Rabbi. White Deer tended a tiny cedar fire at the far end of the lodge. The temperature was very warm and smoke hung hazily in the air. Sage and cedar smoldered like incense on a flat rock next to the altar. WD no longer wore his usual t-shirt and blue jeans, but instead wore a loin skin, his face beaded with sweat as he chanted in native tongue in the flicker of dim firelight.

Virginia motioned to Johnny to sit beside her across from White Deer. Little Feather and Paul quietly sat beside Johnny and Virginia forming a semicircle facing White Deer. Johnny wished he understood the language of the chants that echoed off the hard walls of the room and penetrated his head. White Deer fanned scented smoke through the air with a feather fan. It reminded Johnny of the incense the Catholic priest had burned on special holy occasions in his childhood. The temperature, although very warm, became bearable. Johnny understood why it was sometimes called a sweat or purification ceremony. He wondered if Scandinavian saunas had been derived from aboriginal ceremonies of the Arctic Lapplander. The four of them slowly, one at a time, began chanting along with WD's simple two and three-syllable chant pattern and beating rawhide drums. Johnny last to join in felt self-conscious and tried to shake his feelings of intruding. He didn't belong here he reminded himself. Slowly however his feelings of embarrassment began to fade and he grew comfortable in his new role as their Native American spiritual drama unfolded. So engrossed they became in the ancient ritual, they forgot where they were, what they were doing and even how long they had been there.

Late into the night WD stopped chanting shocking Johnny back to the present. WD looked up then slowly lowered his eyes and he greeted the four of them.

"Many things have been revealed to us while praying here tonight. Johnny, you have come here from far away with a heavy heart. It is necessary that you put your concern into words. Thoughts left wandering alone in your own heart bring sorrow. Pure thoughts are our gift from God and must be shared with everyone. All good changes in our world begin with pure thoughts, a vision. First, a vision is given as a Divine Revelation, a gift of God revealed to the human mind. Each person is given a special purpose for existing and therefore a special, personal Divine Revelation. To create the vision, to make God's revealed desire a reality, we must put the revelation into words, and we must share it.

Once this vision has been shared, passed on to a person who can understand its meaning, then it begins its life as a worldly reality," WD said. "This same process is talked about in Christianity, it is sometimes expressed as: 'Where two or more people gather in my name, I am there.' WD paused to wait for Johnny to gather his thoughts.

"I'm not sure if I am ready or even able to completely voice my vision," Johnny said. "I have always had the desire to make changes for good in the world. Some of my earliest memories as a child were sincere and deep pity for the less fortunate. I now believe in my heart that somehow I must help to reclaim aboriginal lands for American Indians and possibly all aboriginal people around the world. I truly believe that people all over the world are preparing to champion this and other like moral causes. Many things have happened in the past and are happening even now to make these changes necessary and even inevitable."

"The earth has been finally consumed with humanity's lust for material comfort, greed for power and wealth, neglect and self-serving ignorance. Earth's ability to provide for all of life has now been overburdened by one species, humankind. The environment's health will slowly collapse and natural disasters will finally shake loose the existing greed based economic and governmental structures in our world," Johnny's words came easily now.

"It is God's way of correcting abuse and inequities. It happens with any species when they over populate or become poor stewards of their environment. This cycle has occurred many times before, the story of Noah's Ark is such a story." He stopped abruptly, was shocked at the words, their meanings and the fact that they had come from him. The five of them sat silently contemplating Johnny's thoughts, replaying them over in their minds.

After considerable time they began to chant again quietly and to beat the large drum in the center of the room. Then WD held up his hand and they all stopped again.

From several leather pouches, WD began a methodical and precise process of revealing and arranging sacred objects of symbolic value: a buffalo horn tip, a portion of elk, moose, and deer antler, a tiny gold nugget and quartz crystal, an intricately carved stone turtle, a feather, and a seashell. Each object represented part of nature from the ocean to the mountain top. He then placed in front of the altar a personal possession of each of the participants, an act of inclusion connecting each of them, the Rabbi, Little Feather, Virginia and Johnny, personally to the ceremony and the web of life. Not to connect to the web of life is to consider one's self separate, or not personally connected, to all of humanity and nature's living, and the inanimate-that was illusion. Everything is interconnected and to waste even one creature's life was a mortal sin. Then out of respect for his company WD reminded them that in the old testament reference is made to God knowing the number of hairs on a man's head and of valuing even a single sparrow.

"Let us pray and meditate that we may quiet our minds," WD said. "Quiet our minds so that we might listen to God speaking to us, instructing us, so that we can be one with Him who is everything. So that we can be healed of our physical diseases and mental illusions." WD stood and waved the eagle feather fan, blowing the sage into the face and bodies of all.

"Life is a circle," White Deer said, lowering his hand. "Once, America was a great and powerful nation. A nation full of proud and hard working people. It was a nation of great spiritual depth, where moral character was kept in high regard. A land full of compassionate people, who raised families and enjoyed social gatherings within the communities. Family life was central to everything. Americans cared for the land and nurtured trade with other people. America's people were proud and strong, altogether a land that was truly blessed by God."

"Then came a migration of foreign people completely unlike Americans in looks and cultures. The migration changed the course of history. As the immigrants arrived, they looked for a better way of life and found it. America was a new country, full of promise, not saddled with out dated customs and greedy rulers."

"Many of the immigrants had given up everything to come and arrived in America with little. The charity of the American citizens enabled the immigrants to survive and finally thrive in this new land. Immigrants raised families and sent for friends and relatives from distant homelands overseas to share in the great natural wealth of the new land. Eventually the immigrants began to out number the American citizens altering their known way of life."

"The immigrants had different value and belief systems. Not understanding but fearing the Americans made it easy for the immigrants to justify the use of force to begin to plunder American towns much like the Vikings did in ancient Europe."

"The citizens of America, now victims of the immigrants, believed they had the moral high ground. Americans had always been a proud people who put God first in their daily lives. On the other hand, the immigrants practiced strange religious customs. These ungrateful, greedy, land-grabbing, and life-destroying immigrants angered the Americans."

"Wars raged between the Americans and the immigrants with the immigrants eventually gaining control of America, over-powered. The immigrants broke their promises made to the conquered sick and dwindling Americans and continued to push them from their jobs and homes and property."

"The immigrants eventually became so powerful and careless as to threaten the survival of the entire earth. Irresponsible consumption of natural resources, and callous disposal of their waste poisoned the lands, air and waters making them unfit to breathe or consume."

"The conquered American peoples were herded into wasteland encampments and treated like cattle. The vast majority of American men, women, and children were lost to diseases. At times the immigrants deliberately infected the Americans to inflict even more casualties." WD began chanting and beating the drum again and the others joined in.

∾∾∾

A beam of sunlight peeked through the entrance hole of the adobe roof, reflecting off the walls and into Johnny's eyes. It took a while for him to realize where he was. With his eyes still closed, he could hear Virginia's and WD's muffled voices above him. He sat up and looked around the room trying to remember what had happened and what had been said, to make sense of it all.

It was like trying to remember a dream just upon waking. Only bits of a scene would surface and trying to remember all or to make sense of it all was usually impossible. He was sure of one thing though, last night was not magic, it wasn't voodoo or occult, it was spiritual, prayer, meditation, and revelation. He could live with that, he would have to.

Johnny realized for the first time in his life that he knew what God's plan was for him. He couldn't say when it had been revealed to him and he couldn't imagine how it was going to unfold. But for the first time in a long time, maybe since childhood, he couldn't wait to get out of bed and get started. He wouldn't worry about details because he was certain they would be revealed as he needed to know them. Johnny would live each day, one at a time, and right now he needed to get moving.

You can contact the Author: devedrine@yahoo.com